MONSTERS, MAGIC & MOONLIGHT

A LUMOS GEMS CHRONICLES NOVELLA

JoANNA McSpadden

Content Warning

This adult fantasy book contains themes and elements that may be distressing to some readers, including:

- **Violence** (combat, injuries, and monster battles)

- **Anxiety and panic attacks**

- **Mentions of past sexual abuse** (not depicted on-page)

- **Death**

- **Betrayal**

- **Mild explicit language**

Reader discretion is advised. Please take care while reading.

For those who have ever felt like their past defined them—

You are more than what you've endured. Strength is not just survival; it's choosing to move forward, to open your heart, and to believe you are worthy of love, joy, and a future of your own making. This story is for you.

I

The back room in the small apothecary shop was dimly lit, the flickering firelight casting elongated shadows that danced upon the walls. The air was thick with the scent of damp wood and dried herbs, undercut by the steady, nerve-tightening tick of the clock.

Davi leaned forward at a small, cluttered desk, her dark cloak wrapped tightly around her, the hood casting her face in shadow. It was a shield, a deliberate attempt at authority, though beneath it, her chest churned with desperate determination. She prayed the man across from her couldn't see through the facade.

Moments earlier, her brother Alexander had escorted him in, nodding briefly before shutting the door. Now, Davi's pulse thundered as the man lounged back, his fine clothes and indifferent gaze at odds with her humble surroundings. His expression wavered between boredom and faint disdain, and her stomach twisted—he was reconsidering.

He couldn't walk away. Not now. Not when their shot at the Guardian Games rested on his answer. She forced herself to take a steadying breath, straightened, and cleared her throat.

"So, it's William, yes? Here about the open position?" Davi's tone was calm, revealing nothing of the tension simmering beneath her carefully measured demeanor.

"That's right." William's curious gaze settled on her as she lowered the hood of her cloak.

She sat up taller, gathering a pen and paper as though to take notes, hoping the gesture conveyed more confidence than nerves. "What skills do you bring to a monster-hunting team?" she asked, her hand poised to write.

William twisted his mouth with a hint of amusement. "My talents are . . . specific. No lock too intricate, no guard too vigilant," he replied, a smirk tugging at his lips.

Davi's fingers tightened around the pen in her grip. She forced herself to nod slowly, though her pulse thrummed in her ears. Her gaze flicked briefly to the ground before locking back on him, her expression carefully neutral. How had the perfect candidate appeared out of nowhere? "Impressive. Yet, I haven't come across your name in monster-hunting circles."

He tilted his head, a glint of humor in his eyes. "I'm new to this particular line of work, but the fact you haven't heard of me only confirms my covert expertise. The people I work for have a need for someone whose reputation remains in the shadows."

She allowed herself a slight nod, weighing his words. "And your combat skills? The first phase of the Guardian Games is in the arena. We'll need seasoned fighters."

William leaned back, casually crossing his arms. "I'm no stranger to scrapes. Swordplay, dagger work, a bit of hand-to-hand. My specialty is in traps—setting, disarming, dodging them."

Davi jotted down a deliberate squiggle, hoping it made her look both discerning and official, but she already knew she would ask him to join her team. "Any notable jobs you'd care to share?"

William sighed, leaning forward at last, his piercing gaze sharp as a blade. "Have you ever actually conducted an interview before?"

Davi stiffened, a chill prickling down her spine as her mind veered to an unwelcome memory. She was back in that opulent chamber, its tall windows streaming golden light onto the polished marble floor. Before her sat a blond-haired nobleman at an ornate desk, his posture one of languid arrogance. He leaned back in his chair, one leg crossed over the other, fingers toying idly with a jeweled ring on his hand, as though even acknowledging her presence was an indulgence he begrudged.

"Are you here for the *maid's* position?" he asked, his tone as smooth and dismissive as the silk trim on his doublet. His gaze lingered, roaming over her with an unnerving intensity, appraising her not as a person but as an object—something to be used and discarded. His eyes, predatory and deliberate, caught on the curve of her collarbone, then dropped lower, making her stomach churn. The smirk tugging at his lips was a silent promise, and it wasn't a kind one.

Pushing the memory aside, she straightened her posture, willing herself to sound unfazed. "I've been in an interview, yes," she replied, her tone professional, though her voice carried the faintest edge of steel.

William's mouth curved into a faint, unimpressed smile. "Well, I must say, you're not doing a very good job of selling it."

"Selling it?" Davi's eyes narrowed, and she jerked her chin toward him. "I'm the one interviewing you."

"Oh, darling." He tilted his head with a look that verged on pity. "I'm doing *you* a favor by even being here. And you know it as well as I do."

The casual arrogance made her blood surge hot. "And what exactly makes you think that?" She stood, bracing her hands on the desk as she leaned toward him, daring him to answer.

William's smirk only deepened. "Because you can't enter the Guardian Games without a fourth. Isn't that right?"

Davi's jaw tightened as she met his gaze, the firelight casting sharp shadows between them. "And you can't enter without a team," she replied, her voice low and resolute.

He eased back, fingers laced behind his head, a smug grin spreading across his face. "True enough," he conceded, his eyes glinting with mischief. "But for me, all of this is just a bit of sport. So, tell me, can you make monster hunting more fun?"

"Fun?" Davi scoffed, her arms crossing. "You want monster hunting to be more *fun*?" She studied his expression. He wore an air of practiced indifference, but the spark of something sharper beneath it told her he wasn't here for simple amusement.

"Yeah," William said, shrugging with a flick of his wrist as he stood to wander around the room, casually inspecting the shelves. Then he sighed. "That—and the joy of working with your . . . let's say, patchwork squad? Quite the ensemble, I must admit. A one-handed combat specialist, a leader who's barely seen two years in the field, and a witch with talents that, let's be honest, wouldn't start a campfire."

Heat rose within Davi's chest as anger flared, fueled not just by his words but by his sheer entitlement. Her team was capable—more than capable. "Are those the rumors about us?"

"Rumors?" William scoffed, letting out a short laugh. "Rumors would be flattering. I practically had to dig up your name from the dirt after shaking your flyer off the bottom of my boot. No one's heard of you, Davi. Your brother informed me you've been in Gilderon for over a year now? And still—no reputation, no buzz. That doesn't exactly scream 'champion material' for the Games."

"It's difficult to get noticed in such a big city," Davi replied through gritted teeth. She wanted to tell him to get lost, but he was the only one who'd answered their flyer. They'd been searching for a fourth member for months. As much as she hated it, they needed him. If she pushed too hard and he walked out now, her team would be finished before they even got started.

"Which is exactly my point," William said, crossing his arms and turning to face her. "Most teams that enter the Guardian Alliance's annual Games have six or seven members. With a team as small as yours, you need an edge. Something special. There's competition everywhere, and the judges have no shortage of options. If you want a shot, you have to stand out. Make people remember you."

Davi huffed, shaking her head. "We've fought Zomes and Wulverns already. We just need to continue to do good work. People will see our passion and know that we are worthy of being in the Guardian Games."

William's wry smile deepened as he moved toward the door. "Keep telling yourself that, darling."

"Wait, you're just leaving?" Davi asked, moving quickly to step around the desk. She'd tried not to sound desperate, but the strain in her voice betrayed her.

William retrieved his hat from where he'd tossed it on a nearby chair, placing it back on his head with a practiced, dismissive ease. "I came to see if there was, perhaps, something I'd missed. Something that might spark some confidence."

"There won't be many other teams looking for last-minute members," Davi reminded him.

"That may be true, but you see, I want to *win* the Games, not just enter them. You may have guts entering with only four, I'll admit, but nothing to stir the heart. Nothing . . . inspiring," he said, already half-turned to leave.

Davi's heart pounded in her chest. He was their last shot. Unless a miracle walked through that door in the next few hours, she knew their months-long search would end in failure. If they didn't get in this year . . . She shoved down the memories of her childhood clawing at her—the warmth of his inviting smile, the hollow ache of pretending everything was fine, while the sickening dread greeted her every morning.

"There *is* something," she blurted out, the words slipping free before she could stop them. Her breath caught, and she closed her eyes briefly, the weight of what she was about to reveal pressing down on her chest. She hadn't planned to say it—not here, not like this—but desperation had a way of stripping away plans, leaving only raw, trembling truths behind.

Her stomach twisted as the silence stretched, and she hated herself for needing him enough to do this.

2

"Oh?" William paused, glancing over his shoulder. "And what's that?"

Davi took a steadying breath, then opened her eyes, her gaze sharp and resolute. "Not very many people know about this. And as it is our 'edge' as you put it, I'd like to keep it that way."

William's mouth curved into a smile. Davi noticed the way it softened his otherwise sharp features. His dark eyes gleamed with interest, his grin revealing a touch of charm that only deepened her irritation. "Color me intrigued," he said, turning fully to face her, clearly waiting for her next move.

"You must promise that, even if you walk away right now, you won't speak a word of this to anyone," Davi murmured, stepping closer.

"The word of a rogue like me isn't worth much, but sure—you have my word," he replied with a casual shrug.

Davi's lips curved into a faint smirk. "Once you see it, you'll think twice about crossing me."

William's eyes gleamed with anticipation as he tilted his head, gesturing for her to proceed.

Davi took a steadying breath and closed her eyes. Her hands trembled as she reached inward, stirring the dormant power. It awoke slowly, a prickling heat in her chest flooded down her arms toward her fingertips. A surge of adrenaline jolted through her, then a flicker of fear seized her heart, making her gasp.

She despised summoning the magic. It dredged up memories she fought to forget—the lingering touches, the weight of secrets, the cage she'd longed to escape. Once a source of pride, her power now felt like a curse. But she had no choice. She needed it now.

She snapped her eyes open; her focus locking effortlessly onto the energy flickering within the flames of the surrounding candles. The spell was muscle memory now—so familiar she didn't even need to utter a word. Instantly, the candlelight flared. Flames stretched high, transforming into fiery pillars as she drew their power into herself. Her hands trembled uncontrollably at her sides, the raw magic coursing through her like a torrent.

William glanced around, his wide eyes betraying a moment of surprise before a mischievous grin crept across his face, growing wider with every passing second.

"So . . . you're a witch too. Like your brother," he said, his voice laced with a mix of wonder and glee.

Her magic recoiled at his words, the heat of her power cooling into something sharp. But it wasn't finished. She hadn't tapped into it for months, and now it came rushing out, wild and eager. A soft breeze swirled through the room, carrying the floral taste of her magic to her tongue, vivid and intoxicating. It wasn't enough—the power craved more.

The breeze intensified, spiraling into a vortex before her eyes, blurring the edges of the room. She stared, entranced, at the cyclone taking shape. The wind whistled now, building into a chaotic whirlwind that engulfed the tiny room.

A cacophony of crashes jolted Davi out of her trance. The magic had slipped from her control. Bottles toppled and shattered, spilling their contents across the wooden floor. Books cascaded from the shelves, their pages fluttering like wounded birds caught in the storm, and loose pages on the desk swirled in the air.

William ducked, covering his head but never broke his gaze on the chaos unfolding before him.

The shop door slammed open with a deafening bang.

"What are you doing?!" Alexander shouted, his voice edged with panic. His short, dark hair tousled in the wind, and his sharp features were drawn tight with fear. He threw his hands up, shielding his face as sheets of paper whirled past. "Davina, stop!" he yelled again, his green eyes wild.

Davi clenched her fists, wrestling control over the chaotic energy. She grasped hold of the magic's thread and commanded it to stop. Instantly, the wind died, and the cyclone of paper fluttered to the floor. The room fell silent, suffocated in the aftermath. The candle flames had been snuffed out, leaving only a dim shaft of light cutting through the gap in the curtains.

An ache swelled in Davi's chest—a hollowness where the magic had been. Her hands trembled despite her efforts to still them. Slowly, she turned to William, her heart hammering. *Did I scare him away?*

But William was smiling. His face was alight with an unsettling hunger, his eyes gleaming as though he'd discovered buried treasure. Her stomach twisted. *Of course. They're all drawn to power.*

"What were you thinking!" Alexander demanded, storming across the room. His hands clamped down on her shoulders, his brow furrowed with concern.

"I was just showing William—" Davi began, her voice faltering. A sharp pain seared through her arm, and a wave of dizziness made her sway. She reached for the desk, steadying herself. "I wanted him to see what he was signing up for."

"You?" Alexander snapped, whirling on William. His voice dropped an octave. "You made her do this?"

William smoothed his disheveled hair and adjusted his coat. "I assure you, I did not know this was on the agenda. But," he added, his tone light with amusement, "I must say, this job has become far more intriguing."

Alexander's scowl deepened. "You were going to turn the position down, weren't you? You pushed her into this—forced her hand! You . . . vagabond!"

William chuckled, an infuriatingly dismissive sound that sent heat rising to Davi's cheeks. "Is that how you curse?"

"Alex, stop," she interjected, her voice strained. The pain in her arm throbbed, but she forced herself to meet her brother's concerned gaze. "I'm fine."

Alexander hesitated, his hand hovering near her. "Are you sure?"

Davi brushed him off and turned her attention back to William. Her tone was steady now, though her heart still raced. "So, now that you've seen our big inspiring secret, will you join us? Will you become a member of the Fangslayers?"

William's smirk returned, lazy and confident. "A team with two witches? That *is* a rarity." He tilted his head, as though calculating the odds. "Not against the rules, of course, but it's so hard to find magical talent these days. Your team could have quite an advantage."

Her chest tightened as she waited for his answer.

"How could I resist?" he said finally, settling his wide-brimmed hat atop his head. He started toward the door Alexander had entered through, pausing just long enough to glance over his shoulder. "Write my name, William Bresolis, in that little box of yours."

Davi blinked at the name. *A noble surname?*

"And how will we contact you again, Mr. Bresolis?" Davi pressed, ignoring the flicker of concern on her brother's face.

William made a face. "Please, call me Will. All my friends do. And I'll be in touch," he said with a casual wave as he disappeared through the doorway. His voice drifted back to them "We'll gather the entire team soon. Be ready."

The apothecary fell silent again, the heavy quiet broken only by the faint creak of the front door swinging shut.

Relief washed over Davi, and her shoulders slumped as the tension drained from her body. A small smile crept across her face. *Thank God,* she thought, offering a silent prayer to the one Isavarian god.

Across the room, Alexander stood with his arms full of loose papers, his expression unreadable. Davi's eyes darted to his single white streak of hair, a mark of his power that he bore effortlessly, without the jagged black scars that marred her own arms. She hated that she envied him for it, for twisting even the burdens of their magic into something elegant. Of course, he always had excelled at potions too—a safer, cleaner way to practice their gifts.

"I thought you didn't want to use your powers?" Alexander asked, his tone careful but edged with frustration.

"I don't," Davi replied firmly, meeting his eyes. "But he was going to leave, Alex. And we need him."

"You know the risks of calling on too much magic when you're out of practice," Alexander said softly, though his tone carried an edge of warning. "You could summon a DarkHeart."

The words struck Davi like a blow. She swallowed hard, her throat tightening. A DarkHeart. She hadn't even considered the possibility.

Every witch knew the stories—Isavarian legends whispered in trembling voices, meant to scare young witches into discipline. DarkHearts were creatures born of unchecked magic, manifestations of chaos and shadow. If summoned, they didn't just wreak havoc; they consumed the witch who called them, binding themselves to their soul and hollowing them out from the inside.

Davi's jaw tightened. "I know. I'll be more careful," she said firmly, though the sharp pain flaring in her arm made her voice falter.

Alexander's eyes narrowed as he dropped the items he was holding and stepped closer. "Let me see," he said, his voice softening. He carefully turned her arm over, inspecting the black, jagged lines of the Obsidian Streaks that glistened against her pale skin. His lips pressed into a thin line.

"I'll make another potion for you," he murmured, his fingers skimming the air above her wounds, careful not to apply pressure. "Since you won't take the ones from home." He straightened, adding quickly, "Which is fine. But until we find a miraculous cure like the Healing Stone, or something, you'll have to make do with my weaker potions."

Alexander turned to leave, but Davi called after him. "Alex . . ."

He paused, glancing back at her, his expression questioning.

"We're one step closer," she said, her voice quiet but resolute. "We'll make it into the Games this year."

His lips twitched into a small, tired smile. "I know we will."

As he left, the weight of their reality settled over her like a lead cloak. The apothecary barely scraped by, and Davi knew it was her fault. She'd come to the city with grand promises—to secure a job with a nobleman, send money home, and forge a new life for herself in the city. Isavarian Witches were prized in Gilderon, after all. But her only interview had been . . . wrong, leaving her shaken, jobless, and haunted by the memory.

Alexander had never blamed her. He'd fought for their chance to leave the village, sensing how much she needed to escape even if he didn't fully understand why. She owed him everything. Monster hunting, when she stumbled across it, had been her answer—a way to fight back, to carve a fresh path for them both.

Now, winning the Games was their only chance at a better life. Alexander had sacrificed too much already. She couldn't let him keep carrying her.

Failure, though—it gnawed at her. If they didn't win, they'd have to go back. Back home.

The word felt like a curse, heavy with shame and suffocation. Her jaw tightened as she forced the thought away. She couldn't go back. She wouldn't.

3

The leaves crunched beneath her boots, the sound sharp and rhythmic as Davi ran hard, pushing aside the low-hanging branches that clawed at her arms. Ahead, a fallen tree blocked her path, its mossy surface glistening faintly in the dappled sunlight. Without hesitation, she dropped to the ground and slid underneath, her shoulder brushing the damp earth. She stumbled slightly as she rose, but she didn't stop.

A figure loomed ahead, framed by the towering trees, the worn grip of a wooden sword steady in his single hand. Jasper. His sturdy frame was relaxed, yet his stance exuded readiness. His tawny hair fell just past his ears. A jagged scar stretched across his cheek, a testament to the battles he'd survived. The sleeve of his left arm hung loose at the end, revealing the absence of his wrist and hand.

Davi grinned, her breath coming in short gasps. She drew her own practice swords, one after the other, from her belt, the dulled wood worn smooth from use. Their familiar weight steadied her. With a burst of energy, she launched herself over another fallen log as she swung down on him with a powerful swing.

Wooden swords met with a resounding crack. She pressed forward, her dual blades cutting arcs through the air as she attacked again and again. Each strike felt deliberate, honed by the endless drills and instructions Jasper had given her over the past year.

"Don't leave your side exposed," Jasper said sharply, sidestepping her blade and turning to reposition. The empty sleeve of his left arm shifted, catching her attention.

Focus, she told herself, spinning quickly to cover her weak spot. She swung harder, her breaths growing labored. Determination burned in her chest. She had to win this time. A year of training had taken her far, but the Obsidian

Streaks that marred her arms still sapped her strength. No matter how much she practiced, they left her slower and weaker than she wanted to be.

Gritting her teeth, Davi feinted left, then executed a disarming move Jasper had taught her just days before. Her blade darted toward his, aimed to send his weapon flying—but Jasper was faster. With practiced ease, he deflected her strike and stepped in close, using his wooden sword and body weight to throw her off balance.

When they hunted real foes, Jasper wore a shield strapped to the stump of his left arm. In the field, it was an extension of him, a crucial defense. Here, during their sparring sessions, he always left the shield behind. Maybe it was more comfortable for him. Or maybe it was deliberate—a test, forcing her to learn how to face her enemies' vulnerabilities and strengths without relying on assumptions. Or to remind her of what there was to lose.

Before she could recover, Jasper spun, his blade whistling through the air. Davi barely raised her swords in time to block, but his next move swept her legs out from under her.

She hit the ground hard, the breath knocked from her lungs. Dirt clung to her fingers as she clawed for stability. *Damn it,* she thought bitterly, staring up at Jasper's towering form.

He stood over her, his sword poised just above her chest. The medallion he always wore—a simple bronze disk etched with the twisting branches of a tree—dangled from his neck, catching the light.

"You're improving," he said, a smile tugging at his lips as he dropped his weapon and offered her his hand.

Davi scoffed under her breath. It still wasn't good enough. She wanted to lead their team not just with strategy or magic, but with skill—the raw prowess the leaders of every great monster-hunting team had. Those leaders were always blade wielders. But no matter how hard she trained, Jasper was still better. Maybe he always would be.

But Jasper wouldn't lead the team—he refused—and she didn't want to rely on her magic.

Grinding her teeth, Davi took his hand, letting him pull her back to her feet. She brushed the dirt from her clothes.

"You're doing really well," Jasper said, picking up and sheathing his wooden practice sword. His tone was steady, as if sensing her frustration. "You've only been training for a year. No prior combat experience at all; it's impressive what you've accomplished."

Davi shook her head, stooping to pick up her twin short swords. The smooth wood felt cool in her hands, but it didn't soothe her temper. "You still beat me so easily," she muttered, glancing sideways at him.

"I've had the displeasure of too many years of experience," Jasper replied, his voice softening. "The emperor's military isn't exactly forgiving." His gaze flicked to the bronze medallion resting on his chest, the mark of Tykos etched into its surface. "A blessing and a curse."

Davi caught herself glancing at the empty part of his sleeve again, a pang of guilt following quickly after.

"I need to be better," she said firmly, gripping her swords tighter. "If we make it into the Guardian Games, this"—she gestured at herself, frustration bleeding into her voice—"won't cut it. I'm the leader, and I—"

"You don't have to take this all on yourself," Jasper interrupted, stepping closer. He placed his hand on her shoulder, the weight of it grounding her. "We're a team, Davi. You're not doing this alone."

Davi didn't look up at him, but she felt his steadying presence all the same. She didn't know how she'd been lucky enough to find someone like him. Jasper was a walking contradiction—strong, capable, intimidating to those who didn't know him, yet soft, kind, and endlessly patient. She didn't think men like him existed, and it took a long time for her to accept it wasn't some kind of act.

"I know," Davi said, but her voice was quiet and distant, "but we need to win." She looked back at him, meeting his brown-green eyes. "We need this."

Jasper's jaw tightened as he locked his eyes on hers. "I know," he whispered. "I want it more than anything too." His golden-brown hair swept into his face as he glanced down at the stump of his arm, his hand brushing against it absently. "I can't go back to a life of the mundane, Davi. I've tried. I need to fight. I need to use my skills to protect people. To feel . . . useful. This is the only way I know how to do that anymore."

Davi's heart twisted. Jasper reminded her of Alexander in that way—a burning desire to help others, to save them. But while they both wanted to fight for something, Davi just wanted to run.

She couldn't forget how she'd found Jasper—broken and haunted, drowning his despair in the same tavern night after night. At first, she'd only noticed the Tykos medallion, a mark of devotion to the god of strength, courage, and loyalty. It had drawn her attention. But then she noticed more: the way he sat alone, the weight in his eyes, the way he still intervened when bullies targeted weaker patrons, even while his life was unraveling.

The night she finally spoke to him, he'd just been fired from another job. He'd stood up for her when she'd been cornered by a drunk merchant, his quiet strength scattering the crowd that had jeered at her for denying his advances. And then he'd apologized for assuming she needed his help. She'd asked him to stay—not knowing if she should really trust him as easily as she seemed to, but knowing she couldn't let him disappear.

And somehow, they had both found what they needed. He had become her teacher, her protector. And she'd given him purpose again.

They had become close friends. The closest Davi had ever known. She had spent her life building walls, but with him, they'd fallen before she even realized it. And for the first time, she hadn't wanted to rebuild them.

She could sense when the shift started. When what she meant to him changed. When his gaze softened, lingered, as though she were something rare and fragile, something worth saving. But shame crept in at the edges of those moments, cold and unrelenting.

So, she avoided crossing the line. She pretended not to notice when his hand lingered a moment too long or when his words brushed too close to something unspoken. She kept the distance just wide enough to feel safe.

But there were moments—when he stood close, when his eyes caught hers with quiet intensity—when her resolve faltered. Moments when she wondered what it might feel like to step into the warmth he offered, to let herself believe, if only for a second, that it could be right.

But she couldn't.

So, she kept the gap between them, even as a part of her longed to cross it.

Jasper sighed, drawing her back to the present. "But Tykos knows," he murmured. "We'll have to accept whatever comes. Whether or not we get that acceptance letter."

Davi faltered, her stomach twisting at his words. The acceptance letter from the Alliance hadn't arrived yet, but neither had a rejection. She smoothed back the strands of hair escaping her braid, her hand trembling slightly.

"If we don't . . ." she started, hesitating as Jasper turned his full attention to her. The words burned in her throat. "If we don't get into the Games, Alexander needs to go back. And I—" Her voice broke. She looked away as tears pricked her eyes. "I can't."

She didn't need to explain. The look in Jasper's eyes said he already knew.

The Sacred Elders in her village had celebrated her power, but that admiration had turned into an obsession for one in particular. She could still feel his hand on her thigh, the sickening heat of his breath against her neck. Her body trembled as the memory surged, raw and suffocating.

Jasper kept his distance from her, but she felt his calming presence as he softly said, "Moonlight. Remember the moonlight."

The words settled over her like a balm. It was his way of telling her to breathe, to look up. To remember the nights when she would stare at the moon and dream of something better. She had told him once, in a trembling confession, about how sometimes the anxiety would drown her, leaving her gasping for air. And Jasper, in his quiet way, had found this simple lifeline—a phrase so small, yet so powerful. Slowly, the memories faded, his voice anchoring her to the present.

"Our pasts make us who we are now," he said, his voice steady and serious. "We can't run from them, only learn from them. But you never have to go back there. You can stay here with me."

She wished it could be that simple, but staying with him wouldn't be fair to him. Davi shook her head, her lips pulling into a bitter smile. "The shop will close. Alexander can't keep running it. He was always better at potions than anyone else at home, but even he knows this shop has proven to be more work than we can manage. And I was supposed to"—she stopped, swallowing hard—"I was supposed to find a noble to work for, but we both know how that turned out."

Jasper frowned. "We'll figure something out. If a one-handed ex-soldier can find his place in this world, so can you."

She wanted to believe him. But she couldn't see a way without the Alliance.

"Let's head back. You mentioned our newest member has requested we meet tonight?" Jasper confirmed, slinging the strap of his bag over his shoulder.

Davi nodded, and the two began collecting their gear. The wooden sparring swords and ropes felt lighter than the tension still weighing on her chest. She shoved them into her pack along with her arm guards, the rustle of leaves and the distant chirp of crickets filling the silence between them.

The Guardian Games were everything. She needed this. Getting into the Games was just the first step—but winning? That would be her salvation. The Guardian Alliance was her only real chance for a future. The prize money, the steady monster-hunting jobs—it wasn't just about survival. It was about freedom.

Jasper's words echoed in her mind. *We can't run from our pasts, only learn from them.*

But she didn't know how she could ever stop running.

4

Davi chewed on her thumbnail as she glanced around the dimly lit tavern. The hum of conversation filled the room, punctuated by the clink of mugs and the occasional burst of raucous laughter. They didn't belong here, and everyone in the Green Dragon seemed to agree. She could feel their judgmental stares and see their whispered exchanges.

The scrape of a mug sliding across the smooth, worn wood of the table pulled her from her thoughts. Alexander plopped into the seat beside her, his affable grin in stark contrast to her tension.

"Thanks," she murmured, wrapping her hands around the mug. Her eyes darted to a nearby table, where a group of finely dressed men were watching them too closely. She tugged her hood lower over her face.

Alexander raised his eyebrows, leaning back with a smirk. "You've got *such* a warm and inviting presence," he said, voice dripping with sarcasm.

Davi glared at him. "Do you *see* the way they're looking at us?" she hissed under her breath.

"Well, yeah." He gestured lazily at her. "You've got your hood up like you're trying to smuggle illicit potions or something. Try looking less like a wanted criminal."

Alexander wasn't wrong. Reluctantly, Davi pulled her hood down, releasing a few stray strands of dark hair that curled at her temples. She twisted one between her fingers, a nervous habit. Anxiety hummed under her skin like a taut bowstring. They still hadn't received the acceptance letter to the Games, and time was running out. The thought of missing their chance made her stomach roil.

Will leaned back in his chair, tipping it precariously onto its back legs. "So, now that we are all here, can we talk about this name? Fangslayers?"

Davi blinked at him, caught off guard. "What about it?"

"It's a bit . . . terrible, isn't it?" Will shrugged, his tone casual. "I mean, I get every team needs a name, but where'd it even come from? You guys actually slay a lot of fangs, or was it supposed to sound intimidating?"

Davi narrowed her eyes. "Our early work was mostly dealing with Wulverns in the northern forests. The Isavarians have a nickname for them, which roughly translates to 'Forest Fangs' in Akarian. We thought it fit."

"Mostly *you* thought it fit," Alexander interjected with a smirk behind his mug.

Jasper chuckled. "We could've gone with my idea. The Mighty Three. Or I suppose, the Mighty Four, now."

Will snorted, finally letting his chair drop back onto all four legs. "Yeah, I'm really sorry I missed the vote on that one. Mighty Three? That's the kind of name you'd give a traveling puppet show."

Jasper raised an eyebrow. "Are you saying we're not mighty?"

Davi shook her head. "It's not up for debate. Fangslayers is the name, and it's already on the registry. Besides, the name doesn't matter—what matters is what we can do."

Will opened his mouth to respond, but a loud noise near the tavern's entrance cut him off—a loud scrape of chairs, followed by a collective hush.

Every head turned as the door swung open, and a group of figures strode inside. Their armor gleamed in the dim light, each step exuding confidence and purpose.

Davi's chest tightened, her gaze locking onto the man at the front. His golden hair practically shone, and the proud symbol of the Morningfire house—a sunburst emblazoned on his shoulder plate—caught the light. Her stomach churned with anger at the sight.

Charles Morningfire. The man who had looked at her like she was a trinket for his amusement, a plaything he might toy with and discard when he grew bored. She could still feel the weight of his gaze, crawling over her like an unwelcome touch.

Now, he strode in like a conquering hero, his polished half-plate glinting under the chandeliers, his self-assured smile infuriatingly unshakable. Around him, patrons scrambled to greet him, falling over themselves to exchange nods and handshakes, their sycophantic laughter grating against Davi's ears.

Behind him followed a man with curly brown hair in a vibrant doublet, his demeanor far warmer as he bent to greet a nearby table. A man in blue robes, clearly a priest of the water goddess, Revira, trailed behind, his solemn eyes scanning the room with quiet precision. Next was a lithe woman clad in black, her white-blonde hair gleaming like polished steel.

The rest of the group followed in a steady procession. A hulking man with a brutish air shoved past tables, ignoring the stares his size drew, before flopping down in the corner like he owned the place. A dark-haired man lingered at the bar, his sharp nose and pale skin, made his Isavarian heritage unmistakable. He wore vestments of the Silver Conclave, the Isavarian tribe of the inner city of Gilderon. And finally, a slender girl with golden hair and piercing, green eyes glided through the crowd, her movements as light as a dancer's.

Davi's breath hitched as Charles caught the girl's arm, pulling her close. He draped his arm possessively over her shoulders, his laugh echoing across the room as though the entire tavern was his stage.

"The Darkbane Order," Will whispered.

Davi felt a knot tighten in her stomach. Charles Morningfire, the quickest rising Tykerial Guardsman in decades, was now leading the latest monster-hunting group in the city. Their prestigious title was merely a facade, bolstered by the presence of nobles in their ranks rather than any real accomplishments. Jealousy and resentment simmered within Davi.

The crowd seemed captivated by them, as if they had already triumphed in the Guardian Games and saved the city from a fearsome monster. Whispers filled the air about how this was the first time a Tykerial Guard would compete in the esteemed Games since former Tykerial legend, Peter Stonestride, founded the Guardian Alliance.

"Did you know they were going to be here?" Jasper asked Will.

Will shrugged, his expression unreadable.

"The pompous blowhards," Alexander muttered, taking a long swig from his mug.

Davi knew that these arrogant fools, as Alexander had aptly described them, would be their fiercest competition.

Charles, having disengaged from his conversation, approached his table with the golden-haired girl in tow. Davi couldn't tear her gaze away from her. Her hair shimmered like sunlight, even in the dim tavern lighting. Everything about her—her perfect posture, the subtle, unbothered tilt of her chin—screamed privilege, a life free from scars and struggles. A sharp twist of jealousy curled in Davi's chest, darkening, hardening, until it sank into something far more dangerous: hatred.

Then, the man in the colorful doublet turned his attention to their table. His eyes locked onto Will, and recognition sparked in his expression.

"Will?" he asked, sitting up straighter to get a better look at him.

Davi turned to Will, as did the rest of their group.

"You know him?" Davi snapped, her irritation cutting through her words.

Will smiled, his gaze fixed on the curly-haired man now approaching them. "In another life," he mumbled.

"Will," the man greeted again, his voice warm. "It's good to see you, my friend." He glanced around at the rest of the group, a gentle smile gracing his lips. Davi felt a flicker of relief; he seemed amiable enough, despite his association with Charles.

"Henry," Will replied, his smile shifting to one that felt forced. "Fancy seeing you here."

"Who are your friends?" Henry asked, his gaze shifting to each of the others in turn. His eyebrows lifted slightly, his posture open and relaxed, as though he were genuinely interested in their answers.

Will gestured toward each of them. "This is Davi, Alexander, and Jasper. We've been training together for the Games."

Henry's eyes sparkled. "Ah, competitors, then! I must say, it's refreshing to see how many new teams are entering the Games this year."

A spark of pride straightened Davi's spine at being recognized as competitors, but her fingers tightened around the hem of her tunic as apprehension coiled in her chest.

"Well, well, well . . ." a voice purred behind Henry. Charles strolled up, radiating the confidence of someone who expected the world to part in his wake. "Who do we have here?" His smug grin widened as his sharp, invasive gaze swept over the table, settling on Davi.

Her stomach twisted. How many girls had been trapped under that same soul-crushing stare? To Charles Morningfire, they were nothing—fleeting amusements in the gilded bubble of his privileged life.

For a moment, as his eyes lingered on her face, something flickered. Recognition? She shifted, biting her lip and brushing at her hair as if to disappear.

But the flicker vanished, his smirk unchanging. He didn't remember her. Not the clumsy excuse, not her panicked flight from the interview. Nothing. To him, she was just another nobody, as forgettable as the rest.

It burned more than if he had.

"Charles," Will greeted through gritted teeth, his smile impeccably polite.

Charles's lips curled into a smirk as he pieced together who they were. "Playing monster hunters with your little friends now, William?" His mocking tone was sharp enough to draw a few curious glances from other patrons.

"No more than you are," Will replied smoothly, waving a hand dismissively.

Charles chuckled, the sound as insincere as his grin. "I didn't realize you were so desperate. When we turned you away from the Darkbane Order, I thought you'd slink back to whatever gambling den or opium haze you came from. The fallen son of Bresolis," he sneered. "I hear even your father washed his hands of you."

Will didn't flinch, but Davi's reaction was immediate. She stiffened, her gaze snapping to Will as if searching his face for confirmation—or denial. Her questions burned brighter than ever.

Will's face remained a mask of cool indifference, his smirk almost defiant as he met Charles's gaze. "Oh, my interest was genuine. You see, unlike you, I have talent beyond just what my name is. And so do my companions. But I suppose you wouldn't recognize talent if it hit you in the face."

Charles's face darkened with anger, but he covered it quickly, his grin sharpening. "Talent?" he echoed, turning to look at the others. "You call this *talent?* Street scum isn't talent."

Davi began to stand, her anger bubbling over. But before she could rise fully, Jasper leaned forward, his hazel eyes catching hers like an anchor. His gaze, calm and unyielding, held a plea edged with urgency that spoke louder than words: *Stand down. Not here.* Her movements faltered, the tension in her shoulders softening under the weight of his silent command.

"How much did you bribe your 'Order' to pretend to care about the Games?" Will whispered harshly as he stood, his face coming within inches of Charles's. "You're a fool to trust Selene. She will leave you in pieces when she finally betrays you."

Charles shoved Will in the chest, a spark of fury breaking through his carefully constructed arrogance. "You have no idea what a well-oiled team even looks like," he spat before spinning on his heel. "Come, Henry. We sully ourselves by even talking to them."

Henry hesitated, his gaze briefly meeting Davi's. She saw a flicker of regret in his eyes before he lowered them, whispering a polite farewell as he turned to follow Charles.

"This isn't over, Charles," Will called after him, his voice rising above the murmurs in the tavern. "We'll meet again," Will declared, his voice steady and certain, "in the Games."

Charles stopped, turning his head just enough to glance over his shoulder. "The Games? You've gotten an acceptance letter?"

"We will," Will replied confidently.

A slow smile spread across Charles's face as he turned back to face them fully. "Oh, William," he said, his words dripping with condescension. "If you haven't received a letter yet, you never will." He let out a low, mocking laugh.

Davi's chest tightened, a knot of unease coiling in her stomach. *There's still time.*

Without another word, Will picked up his hat from the table, casting a fleeting glance toward the white-haired girl sitting with the Darkbane Order. She met his gaze with a hint of amusement, her smile enigmatic as she watched him turn and stride out of the tavern.

Charles raised his eyebrows, a chuckle rumbling low in his chest as he returned to his group. He slid into his seat beside the golden-haired woman, who leaned in slightly, her expression cool and composed. Davi's eyes locked onto hers, and her heart gave an unexpected jolt. There was something magnetic about the woman, a beauty that seemed almost otherworldly.

But the moment passed quickly, and Davi pushed herself to her feet, unwilling to remain under the same roof as the Darkbane Order any longer. Jasper and Alexander rose with her, and the three stepped out into the city's chilly night air.

Davi scanned the street, bracing herself to question Will. His noble roots could prove to be their greatest liability. But the street was empty—Will was nowhere in sight.

"What was that about?" Alexander asked, stepping up beside her.

"I don't know," Davi admitted, crossing her arms against the cold. "But one thing's clear—there's a lot about our newest member that we don't know."

"We knew he came from nobility, based on his surname," Jasper added. "But it's obvious he's burned bridges in that world. I just hope his past doesn't come back to haunt us all."

Davi turned toward Jasper, her eyes meeting his. The worry etched across his face mirrored her own, doing nothing to settle the unease coiled in her chest. They were already navigating enough uncertainty. A teammate with dangerous enemies was the last thing they needed—and then there was the matter of the letter.

Her thoughts flickered back to Charles's mocking words. Could he be right? Was it too late to receive a letter?

Jasper's gaze lingered on her for a moment before he broke the silence. "Come on," he said quietly. "Let me walk you both home."

Davi nodded mutely, her thoughts too tangled with doubt to argue. Jasper's gaze lingered on her, but she refused to meet it, keeping her eyes fixed ahead. Together, they began the long walk back to the apothecary, their footsteps heavy with unspoken fears. The city buzzed faintly around them, a stark contrast to the opulent warmth of the tavern they'd just left. Davi's mind churned, replaying the evening's events.

The Darkbane Order. They had resources, training, and status. Charles had been raised for this kind of life—trained from youth, groomed by the Hetikan Academy, and now a member of the highest military order, the Tykerial Guard. His team was no less impressive: a priest of Revira, likely a skilled healer, and an Isavarian witch whose powers they could only guess at. The other members were likely at the top of their fields as well. They were formidable, privileged, and used to getting what they wanted without struggle. If they were entering the Games, the Fangslayers had little hope of victory.

As they approached their shop, Davi's attention snagged on a white rectangle affixed to the wooden front door, catching the moonlight. She sucked in a breath. A sudden, terrible thought gripped her. Was this their rejection letter?

Jasper noticed the way she froze. "Davi?" he asked softly.

Alexander caught on, glancing between them. "What is it?" he asked, his voice low.

Davi didn't answer. She strode forward with determination before Jasper could steady her nerves. Her hands shook as she tore the envelope from the door, recognizing the seal of the Guardian Alliance. She broke the seal, her fingers trembling as she scanned the letter for the words she desperately sought.

"Well?" Alexander urged, leaning in anxiously.

Davi didn't reply. Her eyes remained locked on the parchment, her heart pounding, until the meaning of the words sunk in. Slowly, a smile broke across her face, bright and genuine.

"We got in."

5

The city of Gilderon was alive with energy. Excited voices and raucous laughter echoed off the cobblestones as the procession for the Guardian Games began. Flower petals rained down in vibrant bursts, carpeting the streets with color. A lively band marched at the head of the parade, their spirited music carrying above the din of the crowd. Everywhere, faces were alight with anticipation and joy.

Davi adjusted her leather armor, the stiff material chafing against her skin in the heat. She needed the armor to hide her ugly black Streaks, but she also hoped it made her look more official. She wanted to look as fierce as she felt. This was her moment, the culmination of her training and determination. Excitement surged through her veins, mixed with a nervous energy that she tried to ignore. She marched alongside her teammates and the other monster hunter groups selected for the Games.

It was everything she had dreamed. Cheering spectators packed the streets from the palace walls, where the procession began, to the Alliance's fortress on the other side of the city. Davi had never dared to approach the palace before. Its grandeur awed her: towering spires, pristine white stone, and gardens so lush they seemed almost divine. She couldn't help but imagine what it might be like to live there, surrounded by luxury. At the front of the procession, the emperor himself led the way, resplendent in ceremonial armor.

Following the emperor were open carriages carrying current Guardian Alliance members, each one waving regally at the adoring crowds. One day, Davi thought with a swelling sense of determination, that could be her. She could be riding in those carriages, a champion of the Games alongside Jasper, Alexander, and Will.

For now, though, the candidate teams marched behind. A woman in gilded armor plucked a flower from the outstretched hand of a child and tucked it behind her ear, earning a delighted cheer. A man with a broad grin blew exaggerated kisses to the crowd. Meanwhile, others slunk forward with their heads down, as though trying to avoid the limelight.

The Fangslayers were near the back of the procession, seventh out of eight teams—practically an afterthought compared to the Darkbane Order, who was granted the prestigious first position. Davi craned her neck to catch a glimpse of them ahead. They rode at the rear of one of the open carriages, soaking in the crowd's adulation. The sight of them made Davi burn with jealousy. The crowd's love for them was palpable, as though their victory was assured. Why did the Order even bother competing? They didn't need the money, and Charles could likely have any position or title handed to him by his father.

Though she hadn't been able to glean the whole of Will's backstory, she had learned about some of the members of the Order from him: Charles had assembled his team from an eclectic mix of talent and privilege. Childhood friends Henry Sundrian and Lucien Clearrain had been his first recruits. Selene Rivesta, the noble-turned-criminal, was plucked from a prison sentence, a decision that made Will bristle with barely concealed bitterness whenever her name was mentioned. Then there was Igor, the Isavarian witch, coaxed away from the Silver Conclave of Gilderon, and Aldric Stoneheart, the team's brute strength, whose hatred for dragons was infamous among the lower city folk. Finally, there was Eleanor, the golden-haired enigma. No one knew much about her, but she was the darling of the crowd, Charles's radiant right hand.

As the procession continued, Davi couldn't shake the nagging feeling that the crowds dismissed her and her teammates. Did anyone truly believe in the Fangslayers? Did they even stand a chance against the likes of the Darkbane Order?

Davi clenched her fists, pushing back against her doubts. She belonged here. She loved the work—the strategy, the skill, the adrenaline of the hunt. This was her calling, her purpose, and no one could take that from her. Let the Order have their wealth and their privilege. She had earned her place here through grit and determination. That mattered more than anything else.

The roar of the crowd washed over her, and Davi allowed herself a small, triumphant smile. For now, she would enjoy this moment, savor the feeling of pride swelling in her chest. She glanced at her teammates walking beside her, their faces bright with joy as they soaked in the applause. Will, unsurprisingly, seemed to enjoy it the most, waving at the crowd with the confidence of someone who already imagined himself in next year's carriages.

Davi let her thoughts drift for a moment. She pictured herself at the ceremony's end, standing tall as she and her teammates were crowned the victors. The medal of the Guardian Games would be placed around her neck, and this life—this incredible, hard-fought life—would be hers.

Yes, they could win. They *would* win. She had to believe that.

The procession arrived at the gates of the Alliance's headquarters, a towering, pale-stone fortress that loomed above the city walls like a vigilant sentinel. Massive iron gates stood open, flanked by intricate carvings of legendary battles. Statues of past champions and fearsome monsters lined the entryway, their weathered stone faces locked in eternal vigilance.

Davi had never seen the inside before. She wasn't entirely sure why—perhaps it was the intimidating aura of authority that surrounded the fortress, or perhaps it was simply that people like her rarely belonged here. But now, as she passed through the grand gates with her team, awe swallowed her hesitation.

The procession moved along a covered colonnade, its vaulted ceilings adorned with banners bearing the Alliance's crest: a silver shield encircled by a golden dragon. Gas-lit sconces lined the walls, their flickering light casting shadows that danced with the excitement coursing through the air. As they emerged into the arena, the sheer scale of it struck her like a physical blow.

Seats rose from the ground in cascading tiers, stretching high into the sky, a monument to the city's love for spectacle. The most important spectators, like the emperor and former Alliance members, occupied covered balconies draped with velvet curtains, sipping wine as they looked on. Below them sat the nobility, finely dressed in crisp suits and resplendent gowns, the ladies shielding their faces with ornate parasols while the gentlemen tipped their hats.

The Fangslayers marched into the basin of the arena, their boots crunching against the sandy floor. Around them, the cheers of the crowd echoed, deafening and alive with energy. Yet, predictably, the most enthusiastic applause was reserved for the Darkbane Order. Davi glanced at them out of the corner of her eye. Charles waved graciously to his admirers, while Eleanor stood radiant and composed. Henry's smile faltered for a moment, but the rest of the team maintained an air of untouchable confidence.

The current Alliance members—champions from past Games—took their places on an elevated stage in the center of the arena. Davi felt a pang of envy as she imagined herself and her teammates standing there one day. Next year, perhaps. For now, they stood in neat rows with the other candidate teams, waiting.

The crowd settled slowly, and the leader of the Guardian Alliance, Peter Stonestride, stepped forward onto the stage. His silver armor gleamed in the sunlight, an emblem of his legacy as both a warrior and a leader. Stonestride's voice boomed across the arena as he addressed the crowd, the acoustics of the coliseum amplifying his words.

"Let me be the first to welcome you all to this year's Guardian Games!" he declared, his arms outstretched. The audience erupted into cheers and applause, and Davi grinned as she clapped along.

"The most precarious of professions must be undertaken by the bravest and strongest among us. Today, we gather to seek new members for our Alliance. The Games consist of two stages: the arena tournament and the Hunt." His voice was laced with gravitas, and the arena fell silent in anticipation.

"In the tournament, held here in this magnificent coliseum, our eight candidate teams will face off, proving their strength, grit, and cunning. Two teams will emerge as finalists, earning the honor to proceed to the final stage: the Hunt."

Davi's pulse quickened. The Hunt. The challenge that separated champions from pretenders.

"The Hunt is no ordinary trial," Stonestride continued, his tone sharp with warning. "It is a gauntlet of tests—against the wilderness, the elements, and the most fearsome creatures of our lands. This year, we raise the stakes. Our finalists will venture into the lair of a"—Stonestride paused, letting the suspense gather in the air—"rock dragon!"

Gasps and murmurs rippled through the crowd. Even the confident faces of some rival teams showed faint cracks. Rock dragons were a nightmare—massive, armored beasts that could crush boulders with their jaws and unleash torrents of molten breath.

Davi glanced at the Darkbane Order. Charles's smirk hadn't faltered, though his companions betrayed subtle unease. Henry's shoulders tensed; the Isavarian witch stood rigidly straight; even Aldric's habitual knuckle-cracking seemed less casual.

Excitement surged through Davi, untempered by the fear that gripped the crowd. This was the opportunity she had craved, a chance to prove herself and her team against the most formidable of foes.

Stonestride raised his hands, and the crowd fell silent once more. "I must warn you all," he said gravely, "that the Games are not without risk. While the arena matches are conducted with care, accidents happen. Magic is limited to certain spells, and combatants must exercise caution. The tournament matches will be called by judges, and non-lethal force is mandatory. Beyond the arena, however, there are no rules to protect you. The Hunt is real, and failure can mean death. If you cannot handle the Games, you will not survive as members of this Alliance."

Davi's stomach twisted, her earlier excitement dimming. She glanced at her brother, Alexander, standing beside her. His face betrayed no fear, but the thought of him facing a rock dragon made her chest tighten. If something happened to him, she didn't know how she'd recover. Her hands itched to reach out, but she stopped herself. She couldn't afford to look weak, not here, not now.

A flicker of movement drew her attention to her left. Other candidates were whispering, their eyes fixed on her and her team.

"Too small," one muttered.

"How did they even get in?" another added with a snort.

"They don't belong here," came a sneer. "What a joke."

Davi's chest tightened with anger, a flame igniting in her gut. Before she could respond, Will stepped forward, flashing the group an infuriatingly confident grin. He waved cheerfully at their detractors, and they immediately fell silent, awkwardly waving back.

"Do you know them as well?" Davi asked in a low voice.

Will shrugged. "Maybe. I know a lot of people."

"You hear what they're saying about us?" Alexander muttered over her shoulder.

Will's smile widened. "Oh, I hear them."

"And you think it's funny?" Davi asked, incredulous.

"Hilarious," he replied, his voice light but his eyes serious. "They have no idea what we're capable of."

Davi swallowed her irritation, letting Will's words bolster her. He was right. None of these people knew what the Fangslayers could do. She smirked at the thought, her resolve hardening. They would prove everyone wrong.

"So, with all of that ceremony out of the way," Stonestride continued, his voice cutting through the din of the crowd, "it is time for the arena fights to be established. Our current members have ranked the candidate teams. The top-ranked teams will choose their opponents, and their names will be inscribed on the challenge board, tracking each elimination until only two remain for the final. The final battle in the arena will determine who enters the Hunt first, giving that team a heavy advantage in the field."

Behind him, a group of assistants stepped forward, dramatically pulling back a cloth to reveal a massive board. Its brass frame gleamed in the sunlight, and intricate scrollwork encased a central bracket structure. Four blank spaces lined each side, narrowing to two, then one—a path leading to the ultimate showdown.

"The highest-ranked team and the first to choose their opponent is . . ." Stonestride turned and accepted a piece of paper from an assistant. Davi bit back a groan as he paused for unnecessary flair. The paper held high for all to see. Everyone already knew what he was going to say. "The Darkbane Order!" he announced, his voice booming. "Led by Charles Morningfire!"

The crowd erupted in applause, and Davi clenched her jaw, staring resolutely at the sandy floor of the arena. She didn't need to look to know Charles was soaking in the attention like a king addressing his subjects. She could practically hear the self-satisfied smirk in his step as he ascended the stage, waving to his admirers like a hero from one of the gilded statues lining the coliseum walls.

The Darkbane Order moved as a unit, their polished armor and confident strides radiating an intimidating unity. Davi kept her gaze low, her stomach tightening with unease. They were going to pick the Fangslayers. Of course they would. Why wouldn't the strongest team challenge the weakest? It was the smart move, an easy win to establish their dominance. Her heart hammered in her chest as Charles stepped forward, surveying the gathered teams below.

He reached into a pile of polished wooden plaques, each etched with the name of a team, and took one in his hand. Turning it over, he inspected the name with deliberate slowness before speaking.

"The Darkbane Order challenges . . ." Charles's voice carried across the arena like a blade slicing through silence. His eyes locked on Davi's, and a slow smile spread across his face.

Her breath caught in her throat. This was it. He was going to name them.

Charles lifted the plaque above his head, the polished wood catching the light. "The Ravenshades!" he declared, his grin widening.

A murmur rippled through the crowd, followed by gasps of surprise and then cheers. The Ravenshades—a powerful, agile team with a reputation for ruthless tactics—were one of the strongest contenders in the tournament.

Davi's heart plummeted to her stomach as the weight of anticipation drained from her body. They didn't choose them. Her lips parted in surprise, and before she could stop herself, a small laugh escaped. The sound was bitter and disbelieving, earning a raised eyebrow from Alexander.

The sheer arrogance of Charles Morningfire was staggering. He wasn't content to secure a guaranteed win—no, he had to flaunt his superiority by challenging a strong team right out of the gate. Either he believed so completely in the invincibility of his team, or he wanted to show everyone how easily he could dismantle the competition, even the best of it.

Her amusement faded, replaced by a simmering determination. Let him be arrogant. Let him believe he's untouchable. One way or another, she would see him humbled.

She tightened her fists, feeling the coarse fabric of her gloves against her skin. "His arrogance will be his undoing," she whispered under her breath, her smirk returning. She was ready. And nothing—not a rock dragon, not the Darkbane

Order, not the doubters in the crowd—would stop her from claiming her place in the Guardian Alliance.

6

The clash of steel rang out as Jasper slammed his shield against an opponent's hammer. The brute—one of the towering men in the Earthbreakers team—growled as he pressed forward with sheer weight. He drove Jasper toward the circle's edge—a swirling pattern of chalk and bronze inlays. The boundary of the wide fighting circle loomed dangerously close beneath Jasper's boots. The crowd roared in anticipation.

"Hold him!" Davi shouted, her voice hoarse. She darted around another opponent, her sword flashing in the sunlight. Her target—a hulking fighter with a war axe—twisted at the last moment, deflecting her strike with the flat of his blade.

"Not today, little one," the man sneered, bringing the blunted axe down in a crushing arc.

Davi barely threw herself to the side in time, the blade slamming into the ground where she'd been standing. Dust sprayed her face. She rolled to her feet, her heart pounding. Across the arena, Will held another Earthbreaker in a grapple of ropes, but his opponent was breaking free, raw strength overpowering Will's smaller frame.

"Alexander!" Davi cried out.

No answer.

She whipped her head around and spotted him against the far edge of the arena.

A brawler had hoisted Alexander up by the throat, his massive hand clamped around his neck. Alexander clawed desperately at the grip, his eyes wide with panic.

Davi's heart lurched when she saw another opponent step toward Alexander, a sinister grin spreading beneath his helmet as he twirled a shining sword in one hand, the blade catching the light.

Jasper shouted, snapping her focus to him. He buckled under a hammer strike, his shield denting dangerously down the middle. With a mighty shove, his opponent sent him stumbling backward, and his boot landed outside the circle.

A sharp horn blared, signaling the elimination of a fighter. Davi's stomach dropped. Disqualified. Jasper was out for the round.

The crowd roared with approval, but to Davi, the sound was deafening in the worst way. Her eyes darted back to Alexander—his face was red, his hands clawing desperately at the massive hand around his throat. His legs kicked weakly, his movements growing slower.

Panic tightened her chest, a suffocating weight. The judges were going to let him die. His strength faltered, his gasps for air became shallower. Alexander was more important than any competition, any rules, any victory. If she lost him—if he fell here—it would be her failure.

Her pulse thundered in her ears as the chaos of the arena pressed down on her. She couldn't let this happen. Not to him. Not her brother.

For a brief, desperate moment, her mind raced to the power she'd sworn never to use. It prickled at the edges of her fingers, teasing her, promising to end this in a single, devastating burst.

Her fingers twitched, trembling as they reached for that forbidden edge.

No.

Davi froze, her breath catching in her throat. The thought of releasing it here, in front of everyone, twisted her insides into knots. Panic surged. What if she couldn't control it again? What if she lost herself completely and summoned a DarkHeart? And what if she killed Alexander while trying to protect him?

They were outnumbered, surrounded. It didn't matter how clever they were now—raw strength was tearing them apart.

But perhaps . . . perhaps she could use their size against them.

Gritting her teeth, she darted toward Alexander's attacker. She snatched a pouch from her belt and hurled it at the advancing fighter just before he could knock out her brother. The small bag burst, releasing a cloud of glittering powder that coated him in shimmering gold. He froze, blinded and disoriented. He shouted, distracting the brawler still holding onto Alexander, giving him just enough time to kick free from his grasp.

"Thunder, Alex!" Davi called.

Will's head snapped toward her, and he nodded subtly, understanding the coded command instantly.

Alexander gasped, stumbling away from his opponent's grip. His trembling hand shot up as he muttered a spell, and the air crackled with energy.

"Now!" Davi bellowed.

At her cue, Will leapt back, narrowly avoiding the devastating edge of Alexander's shockwave. The blast of energy erupted outward, sending both opponents sprawling to the ground and tumbling out of bounds.

Two horns blared in quick succession.

Will wasted no time. The shockwave had thrown his grappled opponent off balance, and he capitalized on the moment. Tightening his grip, he twisted sharply, sweeping the brute's legs out from under him. A swift kick to the side sent the Earthbreaker skidding across the ground and over the line.

The crowd roared, their cheers rising in a fever pitch, but Davi barely registered the noise. Her chest heaved as her eyes darted to her brother. Alexander was still on his feet, though his shoulders slumped with exhaustion. Relief swept through her like a tide, but she pushed it aside—they weren't finished yet.

Only one Earthbreaker remained, his tattooed frame a mountain of muscle. He roared in fury, charging at Davi with reckless abandon. She ducked his first swing, narrowly avoiding a crushing blow. The second punch grazed her ribs, knocking the wind from her lungs, but she twisted away, using his momentum against him.

"Will, legs!" she shouted.

Will darted in behind the brute, his rope snapping tight around the man's legs. Davi lunged forward, slamming her shoulder into his chest. He teetered for a moment, then toppled backward over the chalk boundary, landing with a heavy thud.

There was a moment of surreal silence as everyone looked on, stunned. Then a trumpet sounded, and the announcer's voice cut through the air. "The Fangslayers are victorious!"

Davi doubled over, catching her breath as the cheers washed over her. Their first win. It wasn't clean, and it wasn't pretty, but it was theirs. Blood trickled from a cut on her temple, and her arms trembled from exertion, but she smiled through the pain. Jasper rejoined them, clapping her on the shoulder.

"One down," William said easily, with a stretch.

Davi looked up at the tournament board, where their name slid into the next bracket.

"Barely," she muttered, her eyes narrowing as she scanned the arena.

Will leaned in, his voice light but pointed. "You know, it wouldn't have been so hard if you'd just unleashed your secret weapon."

Davi stiffened. She glared at him, but Will only grinned and raised his hands in mock surrender. "I just thought I'd mention it," he added, turning his attention to the tournament board.

Their name slid into the next bracket, but Davi's eyes lingered on the Shadowstalkers watching from the sidelines. Cloaked in darkness, their forms were still as stone, but their presence exuded menace.

The next match would be harder. Much harder.

But for now, they had earned this moment.

The arena floor was quickly cleared, the battered Earthbreakers carted off while the Fangslayers limped toward the healer's tent. The healers pulled out fresh bandages and strong-smelling ointments. Davi's arm burned as they wrapped up her bleeding wound tightly. Will's wounds were treated with a special salve while Jasper nursed a split lip, and Alexander still winced with every breath. They would need every ounce of strength for the next match.

Peter Stonestride, strode out to the edge of his balcony above the crowd, announcing the semi-finals. Onlookers were encouraged to stretch their legs, grab refreshments, and place their bets before the final four teams took the stage.

Among those teams was the Darkbane Order.

Davi leaned against a post, letting the healer finish securing her bandage as her eyes drifted toward their corner. The Order's victory in the first round had been swift, so much so that Davi had caught little of it. Jasper, despite his height, said he couldn't make out what happened either, as they were positioned inside the tunnel with the Earthbreakers.

After what felt like an eternity of an intermission, the Order took to the arena for their semi-final match. Davi settled onto the edge of her seat to study them carefully. Learning their strategy would help her team.

Her gaze snagged on the golden-haired Eleanor, the jewel of the Order. Their eyes locked across the space, a silent clash of wills. Davi held the stare, refusing to back down, but Eleanor's expression didn't waver. There was no disdain, no anger—just an infuriatingly calm certainty, as though she'd already won. It was Davi who finally broke the connection, flicking her gaze away.

Eleanor was the image of nobility, from her immaculate armor to her perfect stance. Of course, this competition was probably just another arena for her to dominate, one more trophy to add to her collection.

The horn blew, signaling the start of the match. Davi straightened, her focus sharpening as the Order's members surged forward. The crowd erupted as the team moved like a well-oiled machine, overwhelming their opponents with calculated precision.

Eleanor drew first blood. Her bowstring sang as she released three arrows in rapid succession. All three struck true, dropping three opponents before they could even react. Unable to get up within the five second limit, they were eliminated. The crowd roared, and Davi had to admit—even grudgingly—that it was impressive.

Charles, however, seemed content to linger at the edge of the battle. The smug fighter darted around the melee like a court jester at a noble ball, stepping in only to deliver finishing blows with his polished halberd after his teammates had already done the hard work. Davi frowned, her fingers twitching as she noted his pattern. His strikes were decisive but perfectly timed for show, giving him credit for the last hit without any of the effort.

The fight ended as quickly as it had begun. Charles raised his halberd high over his head and swung it down with theatrical precision, knocking the last opponent unconscious with the hilt. He flipped back his blond hair, flashing a bright, triumphant smile, his white teeth catching the light.

"What a joke," Davi muttered under her breath, smirking as she crossed her arms. The crowd erupted in cheers, oblivious to the pretense.

But the rest of the Darkbane Order was no joke. Eleanor had moved through the battlefield like a vengeful storm, her arrows striking true with ruthless precision. Igor, their Isavarian witch, had been no less terrifying. He wielded his magic with an unnerving ease, his black-clad figure standing unnaturally still as he whispered spells that left his opponents entangled in shadowy vines. Selene darted in and out of the chaos like a phantom, her twin daggers gleaming as she exploited every blind spot. Lucien and Henry played their parts as well, working together to keep the team bolstered and defended. Even their brute, Aldric, with his hulking frame and war paint, seemed almost graceful in his devastating swings, clearing space for his teammates with calculated brutality. The team's strategy was flawless, their teamwork seamless. The Darkbane Order was as deadly as their reputation claimed—except for Charles. A peacock among wolves. His movements were deliberate and flashy, more focused on looking impressive than contributing meaningfully. But Davi couldn't afford to dismiss him entirely. She knew him too well. Charles was everything she despised: entitled, self-absorbed, and oblivious to the struggles of anyone outside his gilded world. Charles might look useless now, but his confidence wasn't baseless. People like him always had something up their sleeves, and she had no intention of underestimating him when the time came.

Her gaze lingered on Eleanor, then shifted to Selene, Igor, and Lucien. If the Fangslayers faced the Darkbane Order, they'd need a plan. Taking Eleanor out early could disrupt the team's cohesion. And if they could handle Lucien or Henry quickly, they might force the rest to play more defensively.

For now, though, she let herself smirk at his preening display. His vanity might just be the crack they could exploit when the time came.

It was time for their semi-final match. Davi's nerves churned, threatening to overwhelm her as she stood to address her team. Alexander handed his team bottles of potions meant to boost their energy levels.

"Just one more battle," she said after downing the sour contents of the bottle, her voice steadier than she felt. "And we're guaranteed a spot in the Hunt."

Jasper leaned on his sword, his brow furrowed. "We'll be against the Darkbane Order in the final," he said. "We need to conserve our best moves. They can't know everything we're capable of."

"We won't get much rest before the final," Davi added, nodding in agreement. "Alexander, stick to the simple spells for now. We'll need your big stuff for the Order, so don't overexert yourself."

Alexander hesitated. "I may have something special up my sleeve—"

"Save it," Davi commanded.

Alexander sighed and nodded.

"We're up against the Shadowstalkers next," Davi said, scanning the tournament board. She turned to Will. "What do you know about them?".

"Me?" Will blinked. "Why would I—"

"Don't play dumb," Davi interrupted. "You know most of the people in this arena. What can you tell us?"

Will sighed, his nonchalant mask slipping. "They're not noble-born, so I know little. But they've got numbers—six of them against us. I've seen an archer and a witch. They'll probably avoid close combat. Alexander should focus on taking them out. The rest of us need to isolate and neutralize the others quickly."

Davi nodded. "Jasper, you'll take the largest one-on-one. Will and I will flank the others, divide and conquer. Sound good?"

Will folded his arms, leaning closer to her. "Sounds good, sure. But are you really saying we're doing this without your powers?"

Davi's eyes snapped to his, narrowing. "We don't need them."

Will scoffed, his casual demeanor evaporating. "That's rich, coming from the one who can't stop shaking. You've got the one thing that could ensure we win, and you're sitting on it like it's a family heirloom you're afraid of breaking."

"It's not that simple," Davi hissed, lowering her voice as the others glanced their way. "I can't—"

"You can't, or you won't?" Will shot back, his voice dripping with frustration. "I didn't join this team out of the goodness of my heart, Davi. I joined to win. If you're too scared to use what you've got, maybe I'm the one who made a mistake."

Her fists clenched at her sides. "We don't need my powers to win this. We've made it this far without them."

"Barely," Will countered. "Isn't that what you just said? And this is only going to get harder. You think the Shadowstalkers or the Order are going to hold anything back? They'll use everything they have to crush us. But sure, let's hope grit and luck are enough."

Davi opened her mouth to retort, but the horn sounded, sharp and unforgiving, jolting her out of her thoughts. She flinched.

Not enough time. They hadn't planned enough. They weren't ready.

But it didn't matter now. It was time to prove they belonged there.

7

The Fangslayers stepped into the arena, the roar of the crowd muffled by the pounding of Davi's heartbeat. Across the circle, the Shadowstalkers emerged from the shadows like living smoke. Clad in black, their features were indistinct, their movements fluid.

Davi's grip tightened on the hilts of her swords. As the second horn blew signaling the start, she tore them free and locked eyes with an opponent. A short sword appeared from beneath his cloak.

The Shadowstalkers moved as a coordinated pack, their movements fluid and synchronized, circling to cut off any escape. Jasper held the largest fighter at bay, their weapons clashing in a symphony of steel. Will darted between opponents, his ropes and hooks tangling between two of them before pulling tight and tripping them both.

Alexander stayed at the circle's edge, sweat streaking his brow as he launched carefully measured spells. A burst of ice shot from his fingertips, creating a slick surface underneath the archer, sending him flying out of the circle when he ran.

Davi moved like a blur, drawing on the energy she'd gained from Alexander's potion, her swords flashing as she traded blows with one fighter. She ducked a slash, drove her blade into his thigh, and spun away just in time to avoid the fighter's heavy swing.

But the next attack came faster than she expected. The fighter, now enraged, swung wildly, his blade scraping across Davi's upper arm. Pain flared as the steel cut through her leather armor. Gritting her teeth, she stumbled back, raising her swords to block the next blow. Blood soaked her sleeve.

The crowd roared as the battle reached its peak. Davi yelled as the Streaks ached and burned on her injured arm. She took a risk, putting her entire weight into a kick, slamming her foot into the fighter's stomach and knocking him to the ground. She spun to see their witch lining up a fiery spell aimed at Will. A ball of flame flew toward him and scorched the back of his armor as he spun.

"Now would be a great time for that special something, Davi!" he called out, bracing himself for another attack.

Davi's breath heaved in her chest as she stared at the witch. Time slowed as the spell left the witch's lips. Davi's powers could be the only answer. But she trembled, and her stomach roiled at the thought.

But then Alexander slammed his hands together, the sharp clap echoing through the battlefield as arcs of glowing energy streamed outward. The energy wasn't a mindless shockwave—it was precise. Each arc split off like a serpent striking its prey, targeting the witch and the remaining Shadowstalkers, sending them all sprawling.

Davi staggered to her feet, her arm throbbing and her chest heaving as though it might burst. For a moment, she feared the battle wasn't over. But none of the Shadowstalkers stirred.

She turned to Alexander, who still stood with his hands pressed together, red energy glowing around his fingertips. Davi blinked, stunned. She'd never seen him wield magic like that before—so controlled, so devastating. He'd been practicing without her. He had seen her freeze, and he'd had to expend a lot of power. She hoped that wouldn't come back to bite them later.

The arena fell silent, the hush stretching long enough for her to wonder if they'd done something wrong. Then the crowd erupted, their cheers washing over her like a wave.

A shaky smile spread across Davi's face as she glanced at her team. She was bursting with pride. When her gaze landed on Alexander, she longed to run to him, to hug him tightly and share the victory, but she stopped herself.

Don't let the Order see. Don't let them know how important he is. Don't give them another reason to target him first.

Instead, she raised a fist to the crowd, letting their thunderous applause swallow her doubts. They'd done it. They had secured their spot in the Hunt and would now battle the Darkbane Order to see who got to enter first.

Davi let herself breathe, but it didn't ease the tight knot in her chest. They needed to beat the Order. The second team to enter the Hunt rarely won—catching up was almost impossible. If they fell behind, it wouldn't just mean failure. It would mean going home. If it came down to deciding if she would use her powers again, she needed to be able to. She needed to be ready.

"Are you ready?" a disembodied voice asked, snapping Davi back into the present.

She blinked and turned to find Will watching her, one eyebrow raised.

"Ready," she muttered, though her voice lacked conviction.

Will chuckled, the sound light but edged with excitement. "You look like you're about to walk into a massive storm."

Davi scowled. "Aren't you nervous at all?"

"Nah," Will said with a shrug, the corner of his mouth curving into a grin. "This is going to be the fun part. The part I'll tell stories about later, mark my words." His eyes flicked toward their opponents, sharpening as he surveyed the other team. "And I know if it comes down to it, you'll do the right thing for the team."

Davi knew what he expected of her. She took a deep breath and tried to steady her nerves, but her hands wouldn't stop shaking. Her arm still throbbed from earlier, and the weight of expectation felt like a stone pressing on her chest.

"The final arena battle is upon us!" Stonestride's voice boomed from his balcony, rising above the crowd's buzz. "Our first finalists and the first to secure their position in the Hunt . . ." He paused for effect, letting the tension build. "The Darkbane Order!"

The crowd erupted, cheers cascading like thunder as the seven warriors stepped onto the platform, their polished armor gleaming under the arena lights. They barely looked scraped up. Their stances were confident, their movements easy.

Davi's stomach twisted as she watched them. Her team had put their all into their last match and had scrapes, bruises, and a bleeding arm. *They're already starting off with an advantage*, she thought bitterly.

"And facing them," Stonestride continued, his tone hovering between exasperation and reluctant admiration, "the most unlikely of opponents—I think we can all agree—the Fangslayers!"

There was polite applause, but the energy was muted compared to the thunderous cheers for the Order. Davi forced herself to walk steadily as she led her team into the ring. She felt every pair of eyes in the arena boring into them, weighing their chances.

The two teams squared off, the space between them crackling with tension. Davi's pulse thundered in her ears as she tried not to notice how easily the Order carried themselves, while her own team seemed worn, beaten, and tired.

Her gaze darted across the opposing team, carefully avoiding the long golden curls of their archer. Davi refused to let her eyes linger there. Seeing Eleanor—perfect, unscathed, and radiating confidence—would only ignite the jealousy and anger simmering just beneath the surface. She couldn't afford that now. Not when focus was everything. Not when letting her wild hatred slip out, even for a moment, might cost them the match.

"Both teams have earned their place in the final phase of the Guardian Games," Stonestride said, his words hanging heavy in the charged air, "but this match will determine who enters the Hunt first—a prize that could tip the scales of victory." He smiled thinly, his eyes flicking between the two teams. "A high advantage."

Davi felt her breath hitch. *We need to win this*, she thought. Not just for the advantage, but to put these villains in their place.

"Let the final begin!" Stonestride roared through the arena as a horn blared, signaling the start of the match.

Davi surged forward, her swords at the ready. Her gaze locked on Charles, who skirted the edge of the chaos, commanding his fighters with infuriating calm. She dashed toward him, determined to close the gap, but Selene intercepted her with lightning speed, daggers flashing in her hands.

Davi dropped low in an instant, as Selene swung her daggers toward her. The blades hissed past her, close enough to draw a line across the torso of her armor.

She rolled to the side, swinging one of her swords in a sweeping arc. Selene leapt back, and Davi gritted her teeth in frustration.

Charles smirked from the edge of the fray, his halberd whirling as he deflected Alexander's bolts of fire with arrogant ease. He even redirected one toward Will, forcing him to duck.

"Alex!" she shouted, raising her blades over head to catch the downward swing of Selene's daggers.

Alexander barked out a spell from across the arena, conjuring a shimmering shield that deflected Selene's next strike. Davi used the moment to roll away, springing to her feet with a nod of thanks in his direction.

Her eyes flicked to Charles again, tracking his movements. He moved like a shadow, always staying just out of reach. She darted toward him, weaving through the melee, but his fighters seemed to sense her intent. Selene and Henry shifted to block her, cutting off her path.

"Coward!" she growled under her breath, spinning to parry Henry's sword. She lunged low, aiming for Charles's legs, but Selene intercepted again, her daggers slashing dangerously close.

Charles's smirk widened as he circled around, gesturing for his fighters to hold her back. "You'll have to do better than that," he taunted, his voice dripping with mockery.

"Jasper!" she called out, hoping to clear some of the pressure. She caught a glimpse of her teammate barreling toward their largest fighter, his sword meeting the man's hammer in a deafening clash. Will moved back-to-back with Jasper. His knives flashed as he parried the less-powerful attacks from Lucien. Will smiled as he emptied a bag of powder into Lucien's face, blinding him and causing him to drop his weapon.

Davi's eyes flashed to Igor, who raised his arms toward her.

"The witch!" Davi called to Alexander as she charged toward Charles again, hoping to catch him alone this time.

Alexander muttered an incantation, and a bolt of light arced through the air, striking Igor in the chest and forcing him to stumble back.

Davi twisted to dodge Selene again, frustration burning in her chest. She still couldn't get to Charles. He was too slippery, always using his team as a shield.

Her breath came fast and sharp as she backed up, her mind racing. Selene's relentless attacks forced her to give ground, but instead of fighting the frustration, Davi let it sharpen her focus. She shifted her stance, feigning a stumble, her shoulders slumping just enough to look tired and vulnerable.

Selene's lips curled into a confident smirk, and she pressed forward, daggers flashing in quick, deadly arcs. Davi gritted her teeth and timed it perfectly—ducking low as one blade hissed past her ear. She dropped into a roll, sweeping her leg out at the last second to catch Selene's ankle. The girl stumbled, her balance faltering for just a moment.

Davi surged to her feet, not hesitating for an instant. She threw herself forward, driving her shoulder into Selene's side with enough force to knock her off course. Selene collided with Henry, their weapons tangling briefly as they tried to regain their footing.

There. An opening.

Davi closed the gap between her and Charles, her swords flashing as she lashed out in a furious combination of strikes. Charles caught her first swing with the pole of his halberd, the sharp clang of metal ringing out. He stepped back to parry her second blade, the force of her strike forcing him to shift his footing. For a moment, his smug grin faltered, his eyes narrowing as he realized she wasn't going to give him room to breathe.

But it was only a moment.

Henry recovered first, his blade sweeping toward her side. Davi spun away to dodge, her frustration reigniting as Selene rejoined the fray, her daggers flashing dangerously close.

"Damn it," Davi growled under her breath, retreating a step. Charles's smug smile returned, sharper than ever, and her chest burned with frustration as his team closed ranks around him once again.

A cry from Alexander snapped her attention away. She turned just in time to see Eleanor's arrow slam into his chest, sending him sprawling to the ground.

"Alex!" she screamed, panic surging through her. Without thinking, she turned and sprinted toward him, leaving Selene behind.

A burning slash across her back stopped her short, pain flaring as her abandoned adversary struck. She staggered but pushed on, stumbling toward her brother. She caught sight of Eleanor approaching Alexander, a rope coiled in her hands and a calculating gleam in her eyes.

"Get away from him!" Davi shouted, but her voice was drowned out by the roar of the crowd.

Her pursuer was relentless. Another strike landed, pushing her to her knees. Gritting her teeth, she spun and drove her blade into Selene's shoulder, forcing her to retreat. Blood slicked her hands as she yanked her sword free and turned back to Alexander.

Eleanor stood over him now, her rope snaking out and looping around his arm. Alexander tried to resist, but he was moving sluggishly, his strength fading fast.

No. This can't happen.

The air seemed to hum around her. Davi felt the magic welling up inside, hot and insistent. She clenched her fists, trying to release it slowly, but the sight of Eleanor lifting Alexander's limp form to push him toward the edge of the circle snapped her control.

With a barely audible word, the wind around her roared to life. Invisible and untouchable, it surged forward, slamming into Eleanor. She stumbled back, her grip on the rope slipping as her eyes widened in confusion.

"What was that?!" someone shouted, but Davi didn't stop to listen.

Eleanor teetered on the boundary, trying to regain her balance, but Davi's magic flared again, stronger this time. The wind howled, an unseen storm, and Eleanor was hurled clear out of bounds, landing hard outside the circle.

Davi's chest heaved as she staggered to Alexander's side. The roar of the crowd quieted as confusion spread. No one had seen the source of the wind—only the aftermath.

"Alexander!" Davi gasped as she collapsed to his side. Her trembling hand pressed to his chest, panic rising in her throat as she felt his shallow, uneven breaths. Relief flickered—he was alive—but he was weakening.

A flicker of movement pulled her gaze. Eleanor was rising, disoriented and unsteady, her eyes locking onto Davi. For a moment, confusion twisted Eleanor's features—then something sharper flashed in her gaze. Recognition.

Davi tensed, her mind racing, but before she could react, pain exploded in her side. She cried out as Selene's blade sank deep, and the rogue's shove sent her stumbling toward the edge of the circle.

"Davi!" someone shouted, but the next instant, Selene's boot slammed into her chest. The world spun violently, and Davi tumbled out of the circle.

The impact rattled through her, sharp pain stabbing through her side and radiating across her body as she landed hard. Gasping, she struggled onto her elbow, wincing as every movement sent fresh agony through her.

From her vantage point, just beyond the edge of the circle, she watched the battle unravel. Jasper stood his ground, battered and bruised, his shield splintered and barely holding together. Will fought desperately at his side, daggers flashing as he parried blow after blow, but their opponents pressed them relentlessly.

Will crumpled first, struck down by Lucien's mace. Jasper was the last of them to remain standing, his roar of defiance echoing across the arena as he swung his sword in a desperate arc. But Aldric's hammer came down one final time, splintering his shield and sending him to the ground.

The horn blared—a shrill, definitive note that rang in her ears.

Davi slumped onto her back, her breaths shallow and ragged. The ache in her side and back throbbed in sharp bursts, but it paled in comparison to the hollow, crushing weight in her chest. Failure seeped into her bones, cold and unrelenting.

Her vision blurred at the edges, the sounds of the roaring crowd fading into a distant hum. The thought of her brother—injured and helpless—cut through the fog in her mind like a knife.

I have to get to him.

She tried to move, to force her battered body to rise, but her limbs felt like lead. The effort was too much. Darkness crept in, swallowing the arena sky above her. Her thoughts scattered, and the ache in her chest dissolved as two words filled her mind before unconsciousness claimed her.

We lost.

8

The memory of the fanfare after the Order's victory in the arena blurred in Davi's mind. She bit incessantly at the inside of her lip. They hadn't even come close to taking them down, and the horror of seeing Alexander shot still twisted her stomach.

The Revira healers had arrived moments after the horn sounded, their swift precision a testament to their skill. One of them knelt over Alexander, working quickly to remove the arrow and stop the bleeding. Another pressed a vial of clear liquid to his lips, tilting his head just enough to help him swallow. His shallow breaths deepened slightly, the tension in his features easing as the herbal elixir began to work.

Davi hadn't protested when another healer forced her to lie back. Sharp stabs of pain in her side were calmed as a salve was spread over her wounds and clean bandages were bound tightly around her. The scent of crushed herbs and a faint whiff of incense lingered in her nose.

Despite their efficiency, gratitude barely surfaced in her thoughts now. A seething rage coiled in her chest, hotter and heavier with each passing second. Eleanor. The archer's face burned in her mind—a calculated, deliberate expression as she released that arrow at her brother. She would pay for shooting Alexander like that.

Davi tasted blood but couldn't bring herself to stop chewing. Her nerves had completely hijacked her common sense. The scene played over and over in her mind, faster with each replay, as she hunted for ways they might have turned the tide.

"Man, what a night!" Will's voice shattered her reverie as the doors burst open, jolting her back to the present.

They were still at the Guardian Alliance castle, tucked into an opulent waiting room with lush couches, armchairs, and tables laden with food. It was a stark contrast to the bruised and battered group it housed. Davi's bed last night had been the most luxurious she'd ever known, but she hadn't been able to enjoy it. She'd spent the night in pain, her mind spiraling between guilt, anger, and flashes of her old teacher's leering smile. She thought of the smug faces of the Darkbane Order, and her fury ignited anew.

Alexander stretched out on a couch nearby, looking far too comfortable. "The most heavenly bed I've ever been in," he said with a satisfied sigh, though Davi saw the faint wince in his face as his limbs extended.

Will plopped into an armchair beside Davi, his usual energy undamped. "What's with you? Didn't you sleep well?"

Davi forced herself to stop biting her lip and leaned back stiffly. "I slept fine," she lied, though her frayed tone made it clear she hadn't.

The door creaked open, revealing a man clad in silver robes adorned with the crest of the Alliance. His stark white hair glowed against his weathered face, the dark lines of the Obsidian Streaks peeking from under his collar. Two guards flanked him, though the man hardly seemed to need them. His stern expression hinted at power and precision.

"The Fangslayers, I presume," he said, his voice clipped and cool.

Davi stood to meet him, holding her side instinctively to ease the pain still gathering there. "That's us."

The man's gaze swept over her with barely concealed disdain before moving to the rest of her group. "It is time for your briefing . . ." He paused, his eyes narrowing as they settled on Will. Recognition flickered—a shadow of disgust. He shook his head, then continued. "Follow me."

Davi glanced at Will, who either didn't notice the reaction or chose not to care. The tension in the air was unmistakable. Will had a reputation that preceded him. And not a good one.

Their footsteps echoed on marble floors as they followed the man through the grand hallways. Sunlight filtered through stained glass windows, painting fractured rainbows on the walls. Any other day, Davi might have found the sight comforting, but her nerves twisted the colors into a blurry mess.

The man led them down a spiraling staircase and into a hallway lined with doors. He stopped before one labeled "Portal Room 5" and turned back to face them. He straightened, his voice formal and impersonal.

"This door leads to the portal that will take you to your starting point in the Hunt. As runners-up, you will enter after the Darkbane Order—hours behind, in fact. Upon entering the room, you will receive a briefing and your allotted supplies before beginning. Are there any questions?"

His eyes swept over them but didn't linger, already distant.

"Uh, yeah . . ." Alexander started. "Who are you?"

Davi tensed. Though she didn't know his name, his silver robes and Obsidian Streaks marked him as an Isavarian witch like them—and a high-ranking one in the Alliance, at that.

The man's smile was thin and humorless as he addressed Alexander. "Alan Markova, Portal Master of the Alliance. A name you will do well to remember."

Alexander opened his mouth to reply, but Davi elbowed him sharply. They couldn't afford to antagonize an Alliance officer.

"If there's nothing else," Markova said, gesturing to the door. His tone made it clear there was indeed nothing else he would share with them.

Davi clenched her fists and stepped into a sparsely furnished room, the faint hum of magic filling the air. At its center stood a glowing, shimmering, blue portal enclosed by an ornate golden frame, its polished surface catching the dim light like a massive, enchanted mirror. A towering man clad in Alliance armor stood behind a golden table to the side of the room, the sigil of the Guardian Alliance emblazoned across his chest.

The door thudded shut behind them, sealing the group inside. The man stepped forward, his presence commanding, with the confidence of a seasoned warrior who had seen countless battles. Scars traced faint lines across his sun-bronzed skin, and his deep-set eyes radiated a mixture of focus and weariness.

"Well met, candidates," he began, his voice a low rumble. "I am Captain Vargas, and I will be briefing you on your mission today."

Davi straightened, her focus sharpening. Every word he said would be critical. She repeated his instructions in her mind as he spoke, locking them into memory.

"Your target is a rock dragon, a massive and ancient beast that has made its lair in the northern mountains of Akaria. As runners-up, you will need to move quickly and with precision, so listen carefully." His eyes scanned the group, pausing just long enough on each of them to ensure they understood the gravity of his words.

"The portal will transport you to the forest lands south of the mountain range. From there, you must track your way to the mountains. Be warned: the forest is home to Wulverns—two-headed wolves known for their speed and viciousness. Stay alert and ready to defend yourselves.

"When you reach the mountains, further challenges await," Captain Vargas warned, his tone grave. "The interior houses a labyrinth designed to test not only your strength but your cleverness and teamwork. Each team must complete a puzzle to unlock their entrance to the labyrinth. Once inside, your mission is to locate and assemble the pieces of a key. Two pieces must be found and combined to form a complete key that will grant you access to the final gate."

He paused, his eyes narrowing as they swept over the group. "There is only one gate, lying in wait at the end of each team's maze. The final gate will open for only one team and lead them directly to the dragon's lair. Once it is activated, it will close behind the successful team. Permanently. You will need to move quickly and decisively to ensure you are the ones who reach this gate first. The team who arrives at the gates second will see a portal that will return them to our fortress. The team who enters the final arena will find an alagon weapon waiting for them on the threshold. Alagon is the only metal that can pierce a rock dragon's scales, so you will need it to defeat the dragon."

He paused, letting the weight of his words sink in. Davi felt her heart race, and she instinctively glanced at Alexander, whose bright eyes hadn't faltered.

"Each of your packs contains enough supplies for three days—no more, no less. Move quickly, or you'll be racing hunger and exhaustion as well as your rivals. Once the dragon is slain and a team's leader secures a dragon scale, a portal will be summoned to bring you back to the castle. Victory and glory await the team that returns with the scale."

Captain Vargas hefted four packs one by one from the ground, placing them on the table with a dull thud. "Take your supplies. Make them last. Use them wisely. And above all, return victorious."

Davi stepped forward, pulling a pack from the table and slinging it over her shoulder. Its weight pressed firmly against her, grounding her amidst the flurry of emotions swelling inside. She nodded to Vargas, an unspoken acknowledgment of their readiness—or her determination, at least.

Turning toward the portal, she hesitated for only a moment. The shimmering surface rippled like water, exuding power. Her heart thundered in her chest as she took the first step. The surrounding air changed instantly, whipping against her skin as she passed through.

A rush of cold overtook her, and her breath left her lungs in a gasp. White light engulfed her vision for a split second before fading into the green of a sprawling forest. Trees stretched high above her and the air smelled of earth and moss.

Davi's eyes darted back toward the portal. It hung, suspended; a shimmering blue patch hovering incongruously in the lush wilderness. She'd grown up in an Isavarian village, trained by the best witches they had, but portals like this were the domain of only the most powerful spellcasters. Her village hadn't seen magic of this caliber in years.

The rest of the group followed her through, each emerging with wide eyes and hushed exclamations. They had no time to marvel, though. As the last of her team stepped through, the portal began to collapse. The edges rippled, shrinking inward until the shimmering light dissolved into nothingness.

Davi watched the display with awe. She imagined Alan Markova, the Portal Master, far away but in full control of this extraordinary feat. Or was the portal self-contained, folding in on itself after its purpose was served? Her mind whirled with questions. One thing was certain: portal magic was an art she knew little about.

She glanced at Alexander, wondering if he might someday master this kind of power. He had been practicing portal magic recently but had yet to master it. If they succeeded, if they joined the Alliance, he'd have the training he needed. Maybe one day it wouldn't be Markova opening portals for them, but Alexander himself.

Davi allowed herself a faint smile, the thought giving her a flicker of hope. That hope would have to sustain her as they moved forward. The forest was vast, and the Hunt had only just begun.

She turned her attention to the nature surrounding them. The sounds of life hummed quietly in the background: the rustle of leaves, the occasional trill of unseen birds, and the soft gurgle of a nearby stream.

Nature had always been her solace, a constant in a world that often felt too chaotic. Here, among the serene wilderness, Davi felt her nerves settle. Everything about the scene exuded tranquility, a stark contrast to the looming danger of the Hunt ahead. She inhaled deeply, letting the scent of fresh soil ground her, and tilted her head toward the sky. The sunlight broke through the treetops in golden streaks, casting a dappled glow over the dark, rocky ground beneath her feet.

Davi dug the toe of her boot into the dirt, marveling at its texture and color—so different from the softer, lighter soil back home. Though she couldn't yet see the mountains above the tree line, she could feel their closeness in the air's thinness and the gradual incline of the land. Her heart raced with a mixture of excitement and trepidation.

This was real. She was here, embarking on the adventure she'd dreamed of for so long. Miles away from Gilderon and her village, she stood on the precipice of danger and glory. Her new armor gleamed in the fractured sunlight, a gift from the Alliance—far superior to the old leather armor she used to wear. On her back were two finely crafted short swords, their hilts wrapped in dark leather. Jasper carried a massive longsword, its blade glinting with an iridescent finish, while Will's twin daggers were sleek and deadly, their edges honed to perfection. Alexander, of course, carried a grand staff adorned with intricate carvings, glowing faintly with latent magical energy.

The very air here felt alive, charged with the thrill of possibilities. Davi could barely contain the urge to sprint into the unknown, to chase down Wulverns, Zomes, or whatever creatures this Hunt threw at them.

"So, I don't suppose you have a plan?" Will asked, breaking the stillness.

Davi blinked, startled out of her thoughts. "A plan . . ." she repeated absently, then looked to the sky, searching for the sun's position.

"I don't see why they couldn't give us a map," Alexander grumbled, folding his arms. "The other team already has a head start. What's the harm in leveling the field just a little?"

"We don't need a measly map," Jasper said, his voice steady. "I've seen Davi track and plan without one before. She'll figure it out."

Davi nodded, though unease prickled at the back of her mind. Usually, she had days to prepare for a hunt—time to scout, gather intel, and devise a flawless strategy. Now, she had nothing but the memory of Captain Vargas's instructions and the rough bearings of the land.

"The mountains should be north," she said, finding the sun's position. "The rocky soil beneath us confirms we are close. Let's head that way and hope for a good view soon."

Without waiting for a response, she began walking, her steps firm and purposeful. The others followed in silence, their trust keeping them close behind.

"So . . ." Alexander began after a stretch of quiet. "You must be some big deal in Gilderon, huh? Everyone back at the castle seemed to know you, Will."

Davi kept her focus forward, but her ears perked up.

Will sighed. "I was once. William Bresolis, of House Bresolis, if that name means anything to you. But those days are over."

"You mentioned a history with that woman in the tavern. Selene?" Alexander pressed.

Will's lips thinned into a grim line. "Selene and I . . . we were involved. Once. But she's part of the reason for my downfall."

"Ooooooh, how juicy!" Alexander teased.

Will's tone hardened. "She pushed me toward ruin. Selene was . . . reckless. Dangerous. I loved her for it once, but she burned everything in her path. Including me."

"That sounds so dramatic," Alexander quipped, earning a smirk from Jasper.

"Alex, leave him alone," Davi said sharply.

But Will held up a hand. "No, it's fine. Maybe it's time we all put our cards on the table. Everyone here has their reasons for being in this Hunt." He paused, as if weighing how much to share. "Selene hated the life we were born into—nobility, expectations, duty. Her rebellious streak was intoxicating. She made me believe we could live free, wild, without consequence. But she had a way of dodging the fallout and one day, she stopped caring about me. If she ever truly did. My choices caught up to me eventually, and I paid the price."

Jasper nodded solemnly. "The past doesn't matter. What matters is that you're here now, fighting with us."

"Exactly," Davi agreed, hoping to quell the talks of their pasts, though a small part of her wanted to hear more.

Will smiled faintly, but Alexander wasn't done. "Still, sounds like—"

A faint click cut him off.

Davi froze, throwing her arms out to stop the group. A chill swept over her, the serene atmosphere turning ominous.

"The trees!" Will shouted, just as an arrow whizzed through the air toward them.

9

"**A**mbush!" Davi yelled, throwing herself toward Alexander and shoving him to the ground just as a bang erupted from where her foot had been. The shockwave sent dirt and leaves flying into the air. She rolled instinctively, shielding her head as more explosions erupted around them, sharp bursts of light and sound that left her ears ringing.

Gritting her teeth, she pushed herself up to assess the damage. Will and Jasper had ducked behind a bush for cover, but Will groaned in pain. Davi's heart sank when she saw him clutching his calf, blood seeping through his fingers from a deep gash.

"Damn it," she hissed, whipping her head toward the treetops where she had caught a flicker of movement. The leaves above rustled faintly, and she spotted golden hair. Eleanor.

Rage ignited in her chest. This wasn't a fair fight; it was a cowardly ambush. She'd used her team's explosive traps to slow them down, but she wasn't retreating. *Her team should be way ahead by now and instead they're wasting time trying to take us out*, she thought angrily. Do they really hate Will so much that they are willing to forfeit a lead just to take him down?

"They must really be worried about us if they set a trap like this," Alexander muttered, brushing dirt off his robes and standing up.

"My damn leg!" Will growled, his voice a mixture of agony and frustration. Despite the injury, he had his daggers drawn, his grip firm.

Before Davi could respond, Eleanor emerged from the shadows, nimble and lethal. Her golden hair caught flashes of light as she leapt onto a low branch, bow in hand and a bandolier of strange metallic vials strapped across her chest.

"Incoming!" Davi shouted, bracing herself as Eleanor loosed an arrow. It flew past her, striking a tree and bursting into a cloud of shimmering, choking gas.

"She's got alchemical arrows!" Will coughed, ducking low. "Keep moving!"

Eleanor was already nocking another arrow, her movements quick and precise. She drew and fired in a seamless motion, the projectile exploding into sharp, crackling shards of energy. Jasper raised his shield just in time, the burst ricocheting off it with a deafening clang.

"Alexander, take her down!" Davi yelled, dodging to the side as another arrow narrowly missed her.

Alexander began chanting, his hands glowing with golden energy. But Eleanor was ready. She grabbed one of the vials from her bandolier and hurled it toward him. The grenade exploded in a fiery burst, forcing Alexander to dive for cover, cutting off his spell.

"Hang it all!" Alexander growled, his robes singed as he rolled behind a boulder.

"I'll draw her fire." Jasper charged forward, his longsword gleaming as he tried to close the distance, slashing through a low branch as he advanced.

Eleanor didn't flinch. She reached into her quiver and pulled a different arrow, tipped with a bulbous red vial. She fired it at Jasper's feet. The ground erupted in a small but powerful explosion, throwing him backward into a tree. Jasper grunted, but his shield absorbed the worst of the impact.

"She's too fast!" Will hissed, weaving between cover as he tried to flank her. "We need to box her in!"

"I'll handle it," Davi growled. Her muscles burned with exertion, but the determination in her voice was unwavering.

Eleanor's sharp eyes flicked toward her, and their gazes locked for a moment. Then the archer smirked and launched another grenade-arrow, this one releasing a sticky, tar-like substance that coated the ground in front of Davi, trapping her boots.

Eleanor smiled with satisfaction, already pulling another arrow.

Davi tugged at her feet, fury rising. The Streaks on her forearms pulsed faintly, a warning of the magic simmering just beneath her skin. She gritted her teeth. Not yet. Not unless she has no other choice.

From the other side of the clearing, Alexander had regained his footing. He thrust his staff into the ground, and a pulse of energy spread outward, shaking the trees.

The shockwave disrupted Eleanor's balance, making her stagger just long enough for Davi to rip free from the tar and close the gap between them. Eleanor recovered quickly, spinning to face Davi and drawing a dagger from her belt.

Their weapons clashed—dagger against sword—Eleanor's speed matching Davi's strength. The archer ducked and weaved, her movements fluid and unpredictable. But Davi pressed harder, forcing Eleanor onto the defensive. A green bauble dangled from Eleanor's neck catching the light with every shift.

Davi's eyes flicked to the trinket, its polished surface gleaming like an emerald beacon against Eleanor's chest. *Jewelry?* Davi thought, irritation sparking amid her focus. *Pretty vain to wear something so flashy during a fight.*

But vanity and privilege weren't enough to save Eleanor now. Davi's strikes grew harder, her resolve sharpening with every swing. The rhythm of the fight shifted; Eleanor was nimble, but Davi's relentless power began to force her backward, step by step, into the defensive.

From behind, Will emerged silently, daggers glinting as he lunged at Eleanor. Sensing the danger, Eleanor dropped to the ground in a roll, avoiding Will's attack. She flipped upright and hurled another grenade toward him, the explosive forcing him to dive for cover.

Eleanor's chest heaved with exertion as she drew her last arrow. This one crackled with energy, its tip glowing ominously. She took aim at Alexander, her hand steady despite the chaos.

"Look out!" Davi screamed.

Time seemed to fracture as the arrow flew, its fiery light carving a path through the air. Davi's heart seized as memories flooded her—the roar of the arena, an arrow piercing Alexander's flesh, his blood staining the ground. Her breath caught, and she was back there again.

But this time, the arrow sliced past Alexander, missing him by inches. The glow from its tip seared through the air before shattering against a tree behind him, sending sparks flying.

Alexander staggered, throwing himself aside, his eyes wide in shock. He clutched at his chest, but there was only the old wound there, still healing beneath the fabric.

Davi didn't care. Panic surged in her chest, her vision swimming as fury and fear took over. She whirled toward Eleanor, her fists trembling. Everything seemed to slow, the world narrowed to a single, devastating question: *What if it hadn't missed?*

A sharp, searing sensation erupted in Davi's arms. Her vision blurred as the Obsidian Streaks on her forearms lit up, purple light burning like fire under her skin. The pain was unbearable, as if her veins were being torn apart from the inside. She screamed, doubling over as the wild magic surged.

A wave of raw, chaotic energy burst outward from her chest, crackling with black and violet sparks. The force swept through the clearing, unpredictable and wild. It slammed into Eleanor before she could react, sending her hurtling backward. Her body struck a tree with a sickening thud, the impact cracking the trunk and eliciting a strangled cry from her lips.

Her bow flew from her grasp, landing several feet away in the dirt. Eleanor crumpled to the ground, clutching at her shoulder, which hung at an unnatural angle. Blood seeped through her tunic, staining the fabric.

The ground beneath Davi trembled, the air rippling with heat and power. She gasped for breath, her arms shaking uncontrollably as the glow of the Streaks dimmed. Her knees buckled, and she collapsed, clutching her forearms as they throbbed.

"Davi!" Alexander called as he hurried to her side.

"What was that?!" Will shouted, dragging himself to his feet and staring at her in shock.

"I—I don't know," Davi stammered, struggling to sit up. Her hands twitched violently, the residual magic making her fingers feel numb and alien.

Davi turned toward Eleanor who was trying to push herself up, her green eyes blazing with determination. But her strength faltered, and she sagged back down, one arm limp at her side. Her breath came in sharp, ragged bursts, and the fury in her gaze dimmed, replaced by desperation as she glanced toward her bow.

Davi's hands trembled as she stood. She reached for her sword and came to stand above the archer.

"Wait!" Eleanor gasped, her voice sharp and panicked. She raised her hands in surrender. "I yield! Don't—don't kill me!"

Davi hesitated, her heart pounding as the adrenaline coursed through her veins. She glanced around the clearing. Alexander stood next to her, hunched but steady, Jasper was pulling himself upright, and Will limped toward them, blood dripping from a shallow cut on his arm.

Eleanor's golden hair was matted with dirt, her face streaked with sweat and dirt. She met Davi's gaze, her green eyes wide and pleading. "Please," she whispered. "I surrender."

10

Davi's stomach fluttered as she locked eyes with the archer. Those green eyes held something unexpected—a flicker of desperation, a profound sadness, and an unmistakable weight of torment.

Her grip on the sword faltered, the blade lowering slightly. She should end this, end her. Right here, right now. Eleanor had ambushed them, had intended to kill them.

And Eleanor had seen the surge of wild magic that had erupted from her. This wasn't the first time the archer had witnessed her powers. Back in the arena, she'd been watching too.

The knowledge this girl carried made her even more dangerous.

Davi's hand tightened on the hilt, her jaw clenching. Her decision was made. She raised the sword again, ready to bring it down on the kneeling archer.

A large, calloused hand gripped her arm.

Her heart leapt in her chest, adrenaline spiking. Without thinking, Davi whirled, her blade slicing toward the source of the unwelcome touch. For a split second, the memory hit her like a blow—rough hands holding her down, pinning her arms above her head. She had been helpless. Powerless.

The blade missed Jasper by a hair as he jerked back, raising both hands, palms out.

"Davi!" he said sharply.

Her wild gaze locked onto him, her chest heaving. Slowly, her mind registered his familiar face, his steady expression. He didn't say a word, only nodded toward the archer and shook his head.

Davi's brow furrowed, confusion flashing across her face. "What? Why?" she demanded, her voice low but tense.

"She's helpless," Jasper said earnestly, his tone low and steady. "She's surrendered. Please, let me treat her wounds."

"You want to heal her?"

Jasper didn't flinch. "I took an oath to serve Tykos. She's no longer a threat to us. We should honor her surrender."

Davi hesitated, turning to the archer. "No longer a threat?"

The girl had removed her quiver and was now pulling daggers from her boots. Davi narrowed her eyes.

The archer raised her hands, dropping the daggers to the dirt. "I surrender," she said again, her voice low but calm, her accent strange and lilting. Her green eyes locked onto Davi's, holding her gaze with surprising steadiness.

Davi let out a sharp breath and turned back to Jasper. "Fine," she muttered through clenched teeth. "You righteous bastard."

A faint smile touched Jasper's lips as he stepped forward, kneeling beside the girl. Davi backed off, shaking her head.

"Bandage her," she commanded. "But don't use any of the potions."

"You're going to let him treat her?" Will demanded. "After she ambushed us?"

Davi's patience was wearing thin. "He'd never let it go if we didn't," she muttered. "Something about an oath to Tykos or whatever. Just let him do his thing."

Will stared at her, his disbelief plain on his face.

"You'll get used to it," Alexander said dryly, clapping Will on the shoulder.

Jasper worked quickly, pulling supplies from his pack and cleaning the archer's wounds. She sat stiffly, her shoulders tense but compliant as he worked.

Alexander leaned in closer to Davi, speaking in a low voice. "We can't just let her go," he murmured. "She'll run straight to the Order and bring reinforcements. Worse, she knows . . . what you can do."

Davi's stomach twisted tighter. She hated that Alexander was right. There was no hiding her powers anymore. And she couldn't forget the pain. It was sharp, searing, and as much a warning as it was a punishment. Her magic was no gift; it was turning against her.

"I know," Davi murmured, chewing the inside of her lip. Her mind churned, grasping for a solution that didn't exist.

"So, what do we—" Alexander began, but Will interrupted, his tone casual yet deliberate.

"If we're going to heal her," Will said, jerking his head toward Eleanor, "we might as well use her."

Davi blinked at him. "Use her?"

"She's clearly skilled—either a highly capable tracker and archer or disposable enough for her team to leave her behind to take care of us by herself. Either way, we can turn it to our advantage."

"You really think she'd help us?" Davi asked, her disbelief cutting through the tension.

"Why not?" Will's expression was maddeningly relaxed. "We're patching her up, after all."

"But we can't trust her," Alexander said firmly.

"Trust is overrated," Will countered with a smirk. "We don't need to trust her. We just need to keep her useful."

Alexander frowned but glanced toward Eleanor. His lips twisted into a dry smirk as he muttered under his breath, "Well, at least they decided to ambush us with the pretty one. She won't be a prisoner who's hard to look at, at least."

Davi rolled her eyes so hard it almost hurt. "Really, Alex? That's what you're thinking right now?"

Alexander raised his hands in mock defense, his smirk lingering. "Just making an observation."

Davi sighed, her gaze flicking toward Jasper and Eleanor. The golden-haired archer was pale but upright, sitting stiffly as Jasper finished his work. She had an undeniable elegance about her—even Davi couldn't deny that—but there were far more pressing concerns than Eleanor's appearance.

Her thoughts swirled. Letting Eleanor go was out of the question; Jasper's oath would prevent her execution, and Will's plan—however reckless—had a certain ruthless logic to it.

"Well," Davi said finally, "she's not going anywhere. Jasper would never let us harm her, and we can't afford loose ends. She stays with us. For now."

She strode over to Jasper, her boots crunching on the forest floor. "We need to keep moving," she said pointedly, her tone leaving no room for argument.

Jasper glanced up briefly, his calm gaze meeting hers. "I'm just about done," he said, cradling Eleanor's arm into a makeshift sling.

"She'll be coming with us," Davi added firmly.

Jasper's lips twitched into the faintest hint of a smile. "That's good news."

Davi huffed and turned away, her resolve hardening as she ordered Alexander and Will to pack up. They'd already wasted too much time. She slung her own pack over her shoulder, the urgency in her chest rising like a tide.

A sudden, sharp pain shot through her arm. Her fingers slackened, and the pack tumbled to the ground. She grabbed her arm, her breath catching as the ache burned like molten iron coursing through her veins.

"Are you all right?" Alexander's voice was sharp with alarm. He was by her side in an instant, his worried eyes scanning her face.

"I'm fine," she lied, forcing a strained smile. She bent to retrieve her pack, hiding the tremor in her hands. "Just sore."

Her brother raised a skeptical eyebrow, his arms crossing. "Stop saying that. You're not fine."

Davi straightened, glaring up at him. "Do you want me to hit you with this bag to prove I'm fine? Because I will."

"I'm just saying, you don't have to pretend. Not with me." Alexander said, his voice lower now.

The sincerity in his voice caught her off guard, and she hesitated, her glare softening for a moment. "I know," she muttered, hefting the pack back onto her shoulder.

The pain had dulled, but it lingered, a cold, pulsing reminder of what she already knew.

She didn't need to look. She could feel the Obsidian Streaks.

The disease that plagued their people, the curse that marked those who dared to wield magic. It wasn't just a warning—it was a death sentence. Davi knew the rules: the more magic she used, the faster the Streaks spread. Three times this week. She clenched her jaw. Of course they'd grown.

Her arm throbbed again, and this time, a ripple of fear ran through her.

The Streaks weren't just a mark of her growing power—they were a sign of how close she was to losing herself entirely. Once, she'd thought she could control it. But now? She wasn't so sure.

Davi approached Eleanor slowly, her voice cold. "You'll stay where I can see you. One wrong move, and you'll regret it."

Eleanor met her gaze and nodded.

Davi glanced at her team, noting their unease. Will was leaning heavily on a tree, still favoring his uninjured leg. Jasper wore his usual calm demeanor, but there was a flicker of concern in his eyes that he didn't bother to hide. Alexander, of course, was watching her like a hawk.

And then there's me, Davi thought bitterly, gripping her arm where the Streaks pulsed beneath her skin.

"Grab what supplies she has left and let's go," Davi ordered, forcing her focus away from the pain in her arm and the roiling nausea in her stomach. She adjusted her pack and began walking, her boots crunching against the forest floor.

Eleanor followed behind, holding her arm still. Davi glanced back occasionally, half-expecting the archer to complain or demand help. Yet Eleanor pressed on, her jaw tight, shoulders squared. Despite the bloodstained bandages wrapping her arm, her posture spoke of resilience.

She's tougher than she looks, Davi thought grudgingly. She'd expected a delicate princess used to easy victories and cushioned battles fought from afar. But now, with the archer's bright green eyes fixed on the path ahead, Davi could see the determination of a fighter in them.

When those same eyes met hers suddenly, Davi quickly averted her gaze, her face heating for reasons she couldn't quite place. She tightened her grip on her pack straps and lengthened her stride, forcing herself to look anywhere but at Eleanor.

Ahead, Will glanced over his shoulder. "Any more traps we should be on the lookout for?" he asked loudly, his tone sharp enough to echo through the trees.

"None that I'm aware of," Eleanor said, her voice soft but steady.

"You sure?" Will replied, clearly unconvinced. "I'd really hate to kill you later if you're lying."

"I am not lying," Eleanor answered, exhaustion tinging her voice.

Will shrugged. "All right. Then you won't mind if I take the lead and check for myself."

Eleanor squinted at him—not in anger, but confusion. Davi frowned. Did she expect them to trust her? What world did she think she'd walked into?

Will moved to the front, crouching low as he examined the ground, trees, and underbrush. His method was methodical, though slow, and he muttered instructions to the group as he went. "Stay clear of roots. They like to rig tripwires along natural paths."

Davi followed his lead, her own eyes scanning the forest for signs of traps. The trees here were denser, their gnarled roots weaving into tangled webs across the trail. Vines hung low, some thorned and others slick with moisture. The air smelled faintly of decay—earthy and wet.

She didn't notice Eleanor catching up to her until the archer spoke.

"You're careful," Eleanor said softly, her voice hesitant, almost respectful.

Davi looked at her sideways. "You say that like it's a surprise."

"Not a surprise," Eleanor said quickly, then paused, wincing as her leg caught on an exposed root. Davi instinctively reached out to steady her but stopped short, her hand hovering awkwardly in the air before she pulled it back. Eleanor seemed to notice, though she said nothing, adjusting her step to regain her balance.

"I only meant you seem . . . capable," Eleanor continued, her tone more measured now. "And focused. A real leader."

Davi's stomach fluttered uncomfortably at the compliment, but she masked it with a dry laugh. "If you're trying to win me over, you're wasting your breath."

"I'm not," Eleanor replied, meeting her gaze again. This time, Davi didn't look away. Something in the archer's eyes—an odd mixture of sincerity and weariness—made her pause.

"I'm just observing," Eleanor added. "It's one thing I'm pretty good at."

Davi huffed, breaking the moment by turning forward again. "Observe all you want. Just keep up."

Behind them, Alexander's voice cut through the growing quiet. "If you two are done bonding, maybe we could pick up the pace?"

Davi rolled her eyes but couldn't help smirking slightly. "Don't strain yourself back there, Alexander. We'd all hate for you to break a sweat."

"Oh, now you've got jokes?" Alexander shot back, sidestepping a thick patch of mud. "Maybe you could save them for when you're not leading us through a deathtrap."

"Fine, next time I'll let you lead," Davi said sweetly.

"Pass," Alexander replied. "This level of dirt doesn't suit me."

Will barked a laugh from up ahead, and even Jasper chuckled softly from the rear.

The brief levity was broken moments later when the trail narrowed sharply, leading them toward a steep incline covered in mossy stone. The sound of rushing water reached their ears—a distant river carving through the landscape far below.

"Careful here," Will warned, his voice more serious now. "This is prime ambush territory. And the footing's bad."

He wasn't wrong. The incline was treacherous, the moss slick and the stones unstable. Each step had to be placed with care, and the added weight of their gear made balance precarious.

Eleanor struggled, her inability to use her arm for balance made her footing even more uneven. Davi noticed her slipping, catching herself against a tree with a wince.

"Here," Davi said brusquely, offering her arm before she could think better of it.

Eleanor hesitated, then accepted, her fingers light on Davi's forearm as they navigated the incline together.

"Thanks," Eleanor said softly, almost too quietly to hear.

Davi was acutely aware of the warmth of Eleanor's touch and the fact that Alexander was watching them from below with an insufferable smirk.

"You're a saint, Davi," Alexander called up.

"Shut up, Alex," Davi snapped, her face heating.

"Just here to cheer you on."

Davi sighed heavily, resisting the urge to chuck a rock at his head.

As they reached the top of the incline, the trail leveled out slightly, but the terrain remained uneven. Will stopped to examine another potential trap.

"We're losing too much time," Davi muttered, scanning the woods.

"Better slow than dead," Will replied, waving the team on.

Ahead, the forest grew darker, the trees thicker and closer together. Davi felt a prickle of unease but pressed forward, the group falling into a wary silence.

She glanced at Eleanor, who was keeping pace now. The archer's determination was undeniable. For the first time, Davi found herself studying Eleanor with something other than distrust.

This wasn't just some hack from Charles's team, she realized. Eleanor moved like someone who'd lived through more battles than she cared to count, her every step carrying a quiet precision that spoke of experience—and perhaps something else. Pain, maybe? Regret?

Davi frowned, the thought catching her off guard. She didn't know a thing about Eleanor, not really. Who was she beneath the sharp aim and a loyalty to the wrong side? A puppet? A zealot? Or something more complicated? The faintest hint of curiosity stirred in her chest, unwelcome but persistent.

She pushed the thought aside, but not entirely. Maybe, just maybe, there was more to her than Davi had assumed.

But trust? That was another matter entirely.

For now, survival came first. Trust could wait.

II

The terrain grew worse as they climbed, the jagged rocks narrowing into a natural bottleneck that forced them to proceed single file. Alexander paused to mutter something under his breath, a small spell illuminating the slickest patches of moss so they could avoid them.

"Could've done that ten minutes ago," Will grumbled as he slipped, catching himself on the jagged edge of a boulder.

"I like watching you struggle," Alexander quipped, his voice tight with focus as he held the spell in place.

For a while, the incline seemed endless, but finally, they pulled themselves onto a plateau at the top. Davi paused, her hands on her knees as she caught her breath. The air was thinner here, colder, and the wind howled around them. As the mist thinned, the northern mountains came into view, jagged peaks rising against the darkening sky.

"There," Jasper said softly, pointing toward the distant silhouette of their destination. The mountains loomed like a promise—and a threat.

"It's almost dark," Alexander said, scanning the horizon. "We should set up camp before we—"

"Wait," Eleanor said suddenly, raising her free hand to stop them.

"What—" Alexander began, but she shushed him sharply.

"Wulverns," Eleanor whispered, nodding toward the path ahead.

The group turned as one, their eyes scanning the trees. At first, there was nothing but the gray monotony of the terrain. Then Davi saw them: hulking forms moving silently between the shadows, their gray fur blending almost perfectly with the stone. Two-headed wolves, their twin sets of jaws dripping with saliva, circled the group.

"They're bigger up here," Davi muttered, pulling a sword from its sheath.

Eleanor nodded grimly. "They grow stronger the farther north you go. These woods are their home."

"Another trick of your precious Order?" Will asked, his gaze never leaving the creatures.

Eleanor shook her head. "No. The Alliance knew exactly where to place this path. At least one team was bound to run into them. The Order probably charged through here and woke them up. Now, they've found us."

"Always cleaning up their messes," Will muttered, pulling out his dagger.

"We need to move as a group," Eleanor began, her voice firm.

"We?" Davi turned to her with a skeptical look. "You think we're going to let you fight with us?"

Eleanor straightened, meeting Davi's gaze. "I want to survive this. I can't shoot with my arm in this state, but I can handle a sword."

"You're not getting a sword!" Will snapped.

"I can't do nothing!" Eleanor snapped back. "You're going to need every hand you can get."

"There's a lot of them. We've never fought this many before," Jasper whispered, coming to stand behind Davi.

Davi held up a hand, silencing them. Her gaze flicked to the Wulverns, their circle growing tighter. "We don't have time for this. Eleanor, you're not getting a sword. If you want to live, stay out of the way or figure something out. Let's move."

"But—" Eleanor started.

"No!" Davi snapped, her eyes blazing. "We're not dying because we trusted you when we shouldn't have. Fangslayers, move!"

With a sharp twirl of her dual swords, Davi stepped into the clearing with the rest of the team at her back. The air filled with the cacophony of growls and the scrape of claws on stone. They moved in perfect synchronization, circling the group with predatory precision, their movements too intelligent for mere beasts. Each beast was the size of a small horse, and their four glowing, yellow eyes seemed to pierce through the dim light, unblinking and hungry. The creatures were massive, their powerful bodies rippling with muscle beneath their mottled gray coats. The largest of them, its fur streaked with silver, let out a howl that echoed across the clearing, signaling the pack to attack.

The Wulverns surged toward them like an avalanche of fur and fangs. Their twin heads moved with terrifying coordination, snapping and snarling as they closed the distance.

Davi met the first charge head-on, her swords slicing through the air and cutting deep into a Wulvern's flank. It yelped but didn't retreat, one of its heads snapping at her legs as the other feinted toward her chest. She danced back, her boots skidding on loose rock.

Jasper's shield slammed into one of the beasts, sending it skidding back. "Hold steady!" he shouted, his voice a rallying cry.

Will darted between the chaos, his daggers flashing. He sank one into the neck of a Wulvern before rolling away from its snapping jaws. "They're relentless!" he yelled, lunging toward another.

Alexander hurled a firebolt that exploded against a Wulvern's flank, searing its fur. It shrieked and recoiled, but another leapt over its fallen packmate to take its place. The tide of beasts was endless.

Eleanor grabbed a broken branch, wielding it like a club with all the force she could muster with her uninjured arm, smashing it into the skull of a Wulvern. The impact staggered the beast, giving Alexander an opening to hurl another firebolt.

Then the silver-streaked alpha leapt toward Jasper. Its massive jaws clamped down on his arm, dragging him to the ground. He cried in agony as blood sprayed across the rocks.

"Jasper!" Davi yelled, her sword flashing as she struck the creature's side.

The alpha snarled but didn't let go, shaking its head and sinking its teeth deeper.

Alexander's voice rose above the chaos as he called to the winds around them. A powerful burst of air slammed into the Wulvern, causing the creature to finally release Jasper, tumbling back with a snarl. Jasper scrambled to his feet, clutching his torn arm. Blood poured between his fingers, staining his armor.

"I've got you covered!" Alexander said, stepping in front of Jasper and raising his hands into the air. "*Shorovit!*" An invisible shield encompassed them, blocking another incoming Wulvern, but he couldn't cast any other spells while he held the shield in place.

The Wulverns kept coming, their relentless onslaught leaving no room to breathe. William's daggers flashed, his movements quick and desperate. "Davi!" he shouted, his voice cutting through the chaos. "We need magic! Now!"

"I can't!" Davi shouted back, her voice trembling.

"You have to!" Will yelled, stabbing another Wulvern. "We're going to die if you don't!"

Davi's pulse thundered in her ears. Another Wulvern lunged at her, forcing her to sidestep awkwardly and twist her ankle. The group was falling apart, their formation splintering as the Wulverns pressed their advantage.

Davi looked at her trembling hands, then at the chaos around her. She clenched her jaw. If she didn't act now, Jasper could die. And if he fell, the rest of them stood no chance. The magic within her stirred, a chaotic force she barely knew anymore. If she unleashed it now, it could destroy everything—and everyone.

Davi raised her hands, the crackle of latent energy sparking at her fingertips. But as she met Jasper's gaze, her breath caught. His expression was hard as stone, his mouth forming a single, silent word: *Don't*. He turned away, reaching into his pack with bloodied hands.

His was face pale and slick with sweat as he gritted his teeth and tore a bandage from his pack. He wrapped it hastily around his arm, blood seeping through the fabric as he secured it. With shaking hands, he downed a potion. Strength returned to his limbs, and he stood tall next to Alexander, raising his sword to the ready.

"Tykos, lend me your strength," Jasper called, his voice booming over the snarls. He raised his good arm, his sword gleaming above him.

With a roar, Jasper charged forward, striking down a Wulvern with a single blow. The beast crumpled to the ground, its heads lifeless.

The tide shifted. Alexander resumed his spells, sending arcs of energy into the pack, forcing the Wulverns to hesitate.

Davi felt a wave of relief, her chest loosening as the group regained its footing without the need of her magic. Her attention flicked to Eleanor, who had edged dangerously close to a break in the rocks—a clear path to escape. For a fleeting moment, Eleanor's gaze darted toward freedom.

"Don't you dare!" Davi shouted, anger surging through her.

The distraction was all it took. A Wulvern lunged at her from the side, its heavy body slamming into her and sending her sprawling to the ground.

Davi rolled, her body sliding across the slick rocks. She tumbled down a short slope, her injured ankle twisting painfully as she landed. Her swords slipped from her grasp as she tried to grab hold of the incline.

Two Wulverns followed her down, their snarls growing louder as they cornered her against a jagged outcrop. She scrambled backward, her hands pressing against the cold, unyielding stone. Her swords lay just out of reach above her.

The beasts advanced, their twin jaws snapping in anticipation. She was trapped. And very much on her own.

12

Eleanor burst into view behind the Wulverns, her face a raw mix of desperation and grim determination. Davi's heart lurched. Eleanor dove for the swords without hesitation, breaking free from the sling that held her injured arm. Her hands wrapped around their hilts tightly. For a fleeting moment, panic coiled in Davi's chest—was Eleanor about to take advantage of her vulnerability? Grab the swords and leave her to the Wulverns? Or worse, finish her off and save herself?

The nearest Wulvern lunged at Davi, twin jaws snapping. Eleanor spun on her heels, the swords gleaming in her grasp.

"Hit the ground!" Eleanor shouted, her voice slicing through the chaos like a blade.

Davi flinched, unsure whether the command was meant to protect her or subdue her. Instinct took over, and she ducked just as Eleanor swung with wild but unrelenting force.

The first blade sank deep into the Wulvern's neck, its momentum dragging Eleanor forward. Blood sprayed in a gruesome arc, spattering her face and armor. The beast let out a strangled yelp, its second head snapping wildly in a futile attempt to retaliate before it crumpled to the ground.

Eleanor staggered, the movement tearing open the wound on her shoulder. Davi saw the bandage darken with fresh blood, and Eleanor's face twisted in pain. But she didn't stop. The second Wulvern lunged at her, jaws wide. Eleanor gritted her teeth and pivoted, her movements clumsy yet fierce. Both blades cleaved into the beast's shoulder, sending it crashing to the ground with a shriek. Its massive body convulsed once, then stilled.

Davi stared, stunned, as Eleanor turned back toward her. Blood dripped from the swords in her hands, and her chest heaved with exertion. Yet, behind the ferocity, something softened in Eleanor's expression when their eyes met.

"Why did you—" Davi's voice faltered, caught between disbelief and guilt for having doubted her to begin with.

Eleanor knelt beside her, holding out the swords. "You needed help," she said simply, her voice steady despite the tremor in her bloodied hands.

Davi hesitated, her gaze flicking between the blades and Eleanor. Then she shook her head. "Keep one," she muttered.

Eleanor blinked, surprised, but nodded. She slipped one sword into her belt and offered Davi her hand. "Come on," she said, gripping Davi's arm firmly and pulling her up.

Davi winced as her weight shifted onto her twisted ankle. Pain shot through her leg, forcing her to lean heavily on Eleanor's shoulder.

"Can you walk?" Eleanor asked, steadying her.

"Barely," Davi muttered through gritted teeth. But with Eleanor's help, she limped back toward the others, each step an effort.

The fight still raged ahead, but the tide was turning. Alexander hurled another spell, his hoarse voice ringing out as a pulse of energy sent two Wulverns crashing into a boulder. Jasper, pale but resolute, roared as he cleaved through another, his blade gleaming crimson under the moonlight.

Eleanor fought alongside them, wielding one of Davi's swords with surprising tenacity. "We're thinning them out!" she shouted, her voice steady despite her bruised and bloodied arm.

Will danced past her, his daggers flashing as he plunged them into the flank of a snarling Wulvern. He spared Eleanor a glance, his expression incredulous. "Davi gave you a sword?"

Davi gritted her teeth, forcing out a reply. "It's fine."

Will rolled his eyes but didn't argue, pivoting just in time to dodge another snapping maw.

The silver-streaked alpha growled low in its throat, its hackles raised, as it surveyed its dwindling pack. With a roar, it leapt toward Jasper, a blur of muscle and teeth.

Davi's grip tightened on her remaining sword. "Not this time," she growled.

Eleanor tensed beside her, ready to intervene, but Davi pushed off her shoulder with a surge of determination. Pain radiated through her twisted ankle, but she forced it aside. With a guttural shout, she swung her blade upward, meeting the alpha mid-leap.

The strike cleaved into its chest, staggering the beast in midair. It crashed down with a howl, just as Jasper stepped forward and drove his blade deep into its side. The alpha let out one last cry before collapsing to the ground, motionless.

The remaining Wulverns hesitated, their glowing eyes darting between their fallen leader and the bloodied but unyielding group. Then, one by one, they melted back into the shadows, their snarls fading into the forest.

Davi lowered her blade, her breaths ragged. Around her, the group stood battered but alive.

"Go!" she shouted after the retreating beasts, her voice cracking. "And don't you dare come back!"

As the adrenaline ebbed, Davi sagged against a nearby boulder.

"You all right?" Eleanor asked softly, her face pale but calm.

Davi let out a faint, bitter laugh, shaking her head. "I thought you were going to run."

Eleanor's lips quirked into a small, wry smile. "I've never been good at running."

For the first time that night, despite everything, Davi found herself smiling back.

"They're gone," Alexander said, his voice hollow with exhaustion. He collapsed to one knee, his hands trembling from magical exertion.

Will leaned against a boulder, wiping blood from his cheek. "Thank Tykos."

Jasper sheathed his sword with a sharp breath, wincing as fresh blood seeped through the hastily-made bandage on his arm. "We need to move before they come back."

"We can't go far," Davi said, steadying herself as she limped toward a flat patch of ground. Her voice, though firm, carried the weight of her own exhaustion. "We're in no shape to keep going tonight."

Her eyes swept the area, catching on a small clearing just off the trail. It was too open for her liking, with little cover, but it was relatively flat—a scarce luxury in this forest.

"There," she said as she pointed. She limped away from the fallen bodies of the beasts that littered the area. "We'll stop here." She shrugged off her pack and let it drop with a heavy thud.

Jasper frowned, his gaze darting to the exposed tree line as he followed her. "Are you sure? We're still vulnerable here."

"We're vulnerable everywhere in this gods-forsaken forest," Davi snapped, her voice sharper than intended. She softened it with a sigh. "Unless you want to carry us all, we need the rest."

Jasper hesitated, then nodded, lowering his pack with a resigned grunt.

As they settled into the clearing, a weary silence fell over the group, broken only by the rustle of leaves and the faint crackle of a quickly built fire. The smell of blood clung to the air, a grim reminder of their narrow escape.

Each of them worked quietly to tend to their wounds. Jasper reapplied and tightened his bandage with a grimace, his jaw clenched against the pain. Eleanor crouched by the firelight, her fingers trembling slightly as she turned her green necklace over in her hands. Her expression distant. Will, seated on a fallen log, pressed a cloth to a bleeding wound on his side. Alexander sprawled on the ground, his chest rising and falling as he caught his breath, the lines of exertion etched into his face.

Davi sat heavily on a flat rock near the fire, leaning her sword against her knee. The ache in her twisted ankle pulsed in rhythm with the throb in her arm from her Obsidian Streaks. She had wrapped her ankle, relieving the intense discomfort, but there was no way to soothe the constant ache in her arm. If she continued to use her power, the pain would get worse; it would never go away.

"We'll take turns on watch," Jasper said, his voice steady despite his evident fatigue. He glanced at Will, who was already setting up a crude perimeter with sticks and stones.

"I'll go first," Will volunteered, brushing dirt from his hands as he stood. His expression was tight, his usual levity dimmed by the lingering threat.

"Good," Davi replied, her tone clipped, though wondering just how the son of a noble came to be adept at setting up perimeters and keeping watch. She shifted her weight gingerly, stretching her legs out in front of her. "We'll head out at first light," she murmured, mostly to herself, though the words carried to the others.

Alexander groaned from where he lay sprawled on his back, staring up at the dark canopy. "If I'm not awake, leave me. Tell the Alliance I died heroically."

Davi chuckled despite herself, shaking her head. "You'll die of laziness long before heroics catch up to you."

"That's the dream," Alexander replied weakly, a faint grin tugging at his lips.

The faint banter lightened the tension, if only for a moment, and Davi let herself breathe, closing her eyes to soak in the fleeting calm. The fire crackled softly, its warmth brushing against her skin. Leaves rustled faintly in the night breeze, and the quiet murmur of her companions' voices wove into the background, reminding her that she wasn't alone.

13

B ut her reprieve didn't last.

Memories surged, gripping her like iron chains. The fire crackled in front of her, its warmth doing little to melt the chill coiled deep inside. Davi sat rigid, staring into the dancing flames, her magic pulsing erratically through her veins. The echoes of its power were a cruel reminder of how it had dominated her. Controlled her.

A phantom sensation caressed her shoulder. A whisper brushed her ear, his voice low and intimate as he held her close.

Her chest tightened. Panic clawed its way up her throat. She couldn't breathe.

Jasper was by her side in an instant. He didn't crowd her, didn't grab her hands or demand her attention. Instead, his voice came low and steady, cutting through the storm threatening to pull her under.

"Moonlight," he whispered, their code word guiding her back to herself.

The haze cracked. The whispers faded. It was always easier to break free of the torment when Jasper was around. If only he could always be there.

"Breathe," he murmured, his gaze fixed on the fire. "You're safe. I'm here."

Davi inhaled deeply, though her breath came out shaky. She forced the air into her lungs again, the sharp chill of the night mixing with the scent of him—forest, smoke, and something faintly herbal, like the salve he always carried for wounds. Jasper had a way of being there for her without making her feel small or fragile. He knew her brokenness but never treated her as less. He never demanded explanations or apologies. It was an unspoken understanding between them, as constant as the stars.

And she wished—God, how she wished—she were strong enough to let herself fall into his arms. To let him truly be the embrace she needed, instead of the anchor she relied on from a distance.

Her breaths slowed, the tightness in her chest loosening as the panic ebbed. She closed her eyes, letting the tension drain from her limbs before glancing at him.

Jasper met her gaze with a soft smile, one that eased the last tremors of fear. His sandy hair caught the firelight, a tousled mess that somehow suited his sharp, angular face. Hazel eyes, flecked with green and gold, watched her with quiet patience. His broad shoulders, sturdy and dependable, seemed carved for bearing weight—whether it was his own pain or someone else's. His one hand rested loosely on his knee, strong and calloused, ready to hold a sword or steady a trembling friend with equal ease.

Davi returned his smile faintly, a silent thank you. Jasper nodded, as if to say, "You're all right. We'll get through this."

His steadiness was her lifeline, her sanctuary in the chaos. And what made it more profound was that he never asked for gratitude. Never asked for anything at all.

"It's surprising she fought with us like that," Jasper said after a moment. His voice was quiet, contemplative. "You said she could've run?"

Davi nodded. "There was a way out. I saw it. But instead . . . she came to my aid."

Jasper nodded again, a flicker of sadness in his eyes. "You should talk to her."

"What? Why?"

"She might be more useful as an ally than a prisoner," he said, his gaze drifting to the girl near the edge of the firelight.

Davi's eyes followed his. The girl who had fought them so fiercely now sat subdued, her expression unreadable in the flickering shadows.

"You go talk to her, then. You're better at that kind of thing," Davi muttered, hugging her knees to her chest.

"She didn't save me," Jasper said softly. "She saved you."

Davi frowned. "She tried to kill us first."

"Perhaps it's not as simple as that anymore. If you don't want to talk to her, at least make sure she doesn't escape," Jasper said as he rose. "I'm going to get some rest."

Davi watched him retreat to his bedroll before shifting her gaze back to Eleanor. Even covered in dirt and blood, the girl was striking—a vision of beauty. Their eyes met. Davi's heart skipped, and she quickly looked away, heat rising to her face.

The others were occupied. Will paced the perimeter, ever vigilant, while Alexander's soft snores blended with the uneasy stillness of the forest.

With a sigh, Davi grabbed a rope from her bag and stood. Her feet felt heavy, weighed down by guilt and uncertainty, as she made her way toward Eleanor.

The girl sat stiffly, her back straight despite the bruises and hastily patched wounds. Her eyes flicked upward as Davi approached, and for a fleeting moment, there was no enmity between them. Just two weary souls, caught in the aftermath of a nightmare.

She stood in front of Eleanor hesitating for a moment as she avoided her gaze, her eyes drifting instead to the green necklace resting against Eleanor's collarbone. It caught the dim light, gleaming faintly. Why does she wear it? Davi wondered, her fingers hesitating for a moment. It must mean something to her.

"I'm going to have to tie you up," Davi said finally, holding up the rope. Her voice wavered, betraying her unease, and she hated how small it made her sound. "Because . . . well, you tried to kill us and all."

Eleanor didn't flinch. Instead, she nodded, dropping her arms behind her back with quiet acceptance. "I understand." There was no bitterness in her tone, only weary resignation.

Davi worked quickly, looping the rope around Eleanor's good arm and moving her injured, bandaged one with careful precision. Then she looped the rope around a small tree behind Eleanor, binding her to the rooted post.

Davi lingered awkwardly, fumbling with the rope's loose ends before finally speaking.

"Thank you," Davi said, her voice hesitant, "for helping me back there."

"It was nothing," Eleanor replied with a faint smile, offering a small shrug that made Davi wince at the strain it must have caused her injured shoulder.

"No, really," Davi insisted, coming to sit in front of Eleanor and forcing herself to meet her gaze. "You didn't have to come back and step in front of the Wulverns like that. You could've run away and let us . . ."

"Let you perish?" Eleanor interrupted, her smile fading. "No. I couldn't."

"Why not?" Davi pressed. "You could've. I saw—"

"And run away, by myself, in the dark forest? The Order has surely moved on without me by now. Unless I'm with you all, I have no hope of getting back to Gilderon. No matter who wins. I couldn't," Eleanor said firmly, her tone cutting through Davi's doubts. There was a shadow behind her words, something unspoken but heavy.

"Why did you ambush us?" Davi asked harshly, blurting out the question with less tact than she had planned.

Eleanor's expression hardened. "Charles," she said flatly. "He's threatened by you. By all of you. The Hunt isn't about fairness—it's about survival. He saw a chance to weaken you before you gained momentum. I was our best option for an ambush. I'm fast, I work from afar, and I know the wilderness."

She pulled her knees toward her chest instinctively, though the bindings kept her arms behind her. Her voice softened. "But I'm glad it failed."

Davi shifted uncomfortably, wishing for the right words. She wasn't Jasper, with his quiet wisdom, or Alexander, who could defuse anything with humor. All she had was her curiosity and a flicker of hope that some understanding might build some kind of bridge.

"You're not from the city?" Davi asked, tilting her head. "With a name like Eleanor, I thought—"

Eleanor's laugh startled her, soft and surprisingly warm. "My name's not Eleanor," she said, a faint smirk tugging at her lips. "Charles gave me that name. Said it made me sound more . . . noble. My real name is Elara."

Elara. The name shimmered in Davi's mind, untamed and fierce, like the girl herself.

Davi's brow furrowed. "He changed your name?" Her voice carried an edge of indignation. "Charles doesn't own you."

"In a way, he does," Elara said quietly, the smirk fading. "But he's promised me something important."

"Winning the Games?" Davi guessed.

"That's just the beginning," Elara admitted, her gaze drifting to the fire. "We need the Alliance's resources. There's something I have to find, and time is running out."

Suspicion prickled in Davi's mind. What was Charles looking for? What could possibly bind a girl like Elara to him?

"You choose to follow him?" Davi asked carefully.

Elara hesitated before shrugging. "I don't have a choice."

The words hung between them, heavy and tense.

After a long silence, Elara turned the question back on her. "Why are you in the Games?" Her voice was soft, like the whisper of leaves in the wind.

Davi froze, her throat tightening. "I can't go back," she admitted, her voice raw. "I need the jobs the Alliance offers. I can't return to my village. I can't face . . ." She trailed off, the words crumbling under the weight of old wounds.

For a moment, Elara's boot brushed Davi's knee. Davi stiffened at first, unaccustomed to touch, but there was something different about the contact—it was steady, grounding.

"Thank you," Elara said softly. "For sparing me. For listening. People don't usually listen."

Davi's smile was small but real. "You're not alone. Not if you don't want to be."

She was surprised by how natural the words felt, as though they'd been waiting for her to say them.

Elara's answering smile was radiant, chasing away the shadows for a fleeting moment.

Davi rose slowly. "We'll leave at sunrise. It'd be good to have you with us."

Elara nodded. "I'd like that."

As Davi walked back to her bedroll, her thoughts churned. The girl she'd first seen had seemed privileged and untouchable. The warrior she'd faced had been fierce and unyielding. But this Elara—vulnerable, complex, determined—was something else entirely.

The fire crackled softly as Davi settled into her place, hugging herself against the chill. She stared into the flames, questions echoing in her mind: *Why do I feel like I need to know her? Why am I so drawn to her?*

14

Davi woke the next morning on the cold, uneven ground, her back stiff and aching. Still, she noted, with some relief, that her ankle throbbed less than it had the night before.

Blinking sleep from her eyes, she scanned their makeshift camp. Her brother, Alexander, was munching on a ration bar from his pack. Will lay sprawled nearby, still fast asleep, his breathing slow and steady. Even Elara remained tied to the tree, her sunshine hair tumbling over her shoulders as she rested against the bark, unmoving.

Davi's thoughts wandered back to the previous night. The memory of Elara's piercing green eyes sent a flutter through her chest, quick and sharp, like a bird startled into flight. Her words echoed in Davi's mind. Charles had something over her. But what? Before she could dwell on it further, she noticed something—or rather, someone—was missing.

Jasper.

Her heart sank as she sprang to her feet, wincing slightly when she put weight on her ankle. She scanned the area frantically.

"Where's Jasper?" she demanded, her voice tinged with rising fear.

Alexander only shrugged, unbothered, while Will groaned at the interruption to his sleep and rubbed at his eyes, his expression groggy and unconcerned. Davi's gaze flitted to Elara, but she quickly looked away. Relief flooded through her as she finally caught sight of Jasper's tall frame emerging from the tree line, his heavy boots crunching on the leaf-laden ground.

"Jasper, there you are!" Davi exclaimed, the tension in her chest loosening. "You scared me."

He stopped and offered a sheepish smile. "Didn't mean to. I told Alexander to let you know I'd be right back if you woke up."

Davi turned a sharp glare on her brother.

"Oh, that's right," Alexander said, chuckling as if he'd only just remembered.

Davi huffed, kicking a loose rock in his direction.

Jasper chuckled, running a hand through his disheveled hair. "I wanted to scout ahead now that it's light. Good news—it looks like our path is clear."

With that, they quickly packed up their belongings. Davi approached Elara, crouching to untie the ropes binding her wrists. Her hands trembled slightly as she worked the knot loose, revealing angry red marks on Elara's pale skin. Elara flexed her fingers but said nothing, her expression unreadable.

"Should we really untie her?" Will asked, standing nearby with his arms crossed. "Might be safer to keep her tied up."

"There's no need for that," Elara said coolly, meeting Will's gaze without flinching. "I'm not going anywhere."

Davi hesitated, her eyes flicking between Will and Elara. She didn't want to look weak—not now. "We'll keep her bound," she said firmly, looping the ropes back around Elara's wrists, though looser this time. "Just in case."

Elara arched an eyebrow but didn't protest, allowing Davi to secure her.

"Her real name is Elara, by the way," Davi mentioned to the group as she turned away from the girl quickly.

Will snorted. "Elara. Hm. Not a very noble name."

As the group set off, Davi fell into step near the back, her gaze drawn to Elara despite herself. Something about her was magnetic, her calm composure undercut by an edge of danger.

"Really, Davina? Her?" Alexander's teasing voice broke into her thoughts. He sidled up to her, a sly grin tugging at his lips. "I really hope you know what you're doing, falling for an enemy . . ."

"I'm not falling for anyone," Davi said quickly, her face heating.

"Sure," Alexander drawled, rolling his eyes. "I'm sure that look means nothing at all."

Davi scowled at Alexander before walking faster to lead the group at Jasper's side.

The group trudged onward, the towering shadow of the mountain growing larger with every step. The morning chill lingered, nipping at their fingers and toes, but sweat dampened Davi's back from the exertion. When they finally reached the base of the mountain, its jagged peaks seemed to claw at the sky, cutting sharp lines into the horizon.

Davi's breath hitched as they neared the smooth rock face. The surface shimmered faintly in the sunlight, and two symbols stood out against the gray stone, about twenty feet apart: a vivid blue spiral and a faded red handprint. The red handprint was dull—almost ghostly—its edges blurred. Unlike the blue spiral, the ground in front of the handprint was bare, without a single stone in sight.

"A symbol for each team," Davi murmured, her voice barely above a whisper. The memory of Captain Vargas's gruff tone surged to the forefront of her mind. "Each team must unlock their own entrance to the labyrinth." Her stomach tightened. The faded red handprint could only mean one thing: the Darkbane Order had already solved their puzzle. They were inside.

"We need to follow the blue spiral," Davi said, shaking off her unease. She touched her pack instinctively, feeling the embroidered patch with the same symbol. Their path had been chosen for them. She pointed toward the vibrant spiral on the stone. "This is our way in."

The others clustered around, the tension between them almost crackling in the crisp morning air.

"Great," Alexander said, stepping up to the wall. With a dramatic flourish, he slapped his palm against the blue swirl. "So, where's the door?"

"There isn't one," Jasper said, frowning as he ran his hand along the cold, unyielding rock. His fingers traced the faint ridges of the swirl but found nothing resembling a seam or handle. "Not yet, at least. Looks like we've got some work to do."

Will stepped closer to examine the sigil. "I've seen something like this before during one of my heists."

Everyone stared at him.

He shrugged, unbothered by their surprise. "Oh, don't look so shocked. We all know my background isn't exactly squeaky clean. Puzzles like this? Kind of my thing."

Alexander snorted, leaning against the wall. "So, what you're saying is, you're a glorified lockpick?"

"Call it what you want," Will said, not missing a beat, "but I've cracked a lot of vaults in my time. And if this is anything like those, the answer isn't just lying around. It'll take some thinking."

Davi raised an eyebrow, gesturing toward the stones. "All right, smart guy. Got any bright ideas?"

His grin widened. "Oh, I've got a few." He brushed the dirt from his hands. "This symbol," he said, pointing to the glowing, blue swirl etched into the mountain, "has got to be the key."

Jasper knelt by the stones at the base of the wall, frowning. "These rocks are too deliberately placed to just be debris. They're part of whatever's keeping the entrance sealed."

Alexander came forward to examine the symbol. "There's definitely magic coming from this symbol. I can feel it."

Will crossed his arms, glaring at the swirl. "Why not just destroy the symbol? You know, brute force."

Alexander gave him a dry look. "Because it's magic, not a trapdoor. You can't just punch a spell."

Davi crouched by the stones on the ground around them, inspecting them. She ran her fingers over one of the smoother surfaces and froze. There was a faint marking carved into the rock—a swirl, identical to the symbol on the mountain. "Look at this," she said, motioning to the others. "These rocks have markings on them too."

Will's eyes lit up as he crouched beside her. "Interesting. We might need to match them up somehow." He grabbed another rock and turned it over. This one had a different marking, almost like a crescent moon. "Different symbols. It must be a pattern."

Davi took Will's rock in her hand to examine it. "They're not just random symbols. They're part of an old language." Her eyes flicked toward the rocks. "The spell on that door isn't bound by the rocks. It's tied to a phrase."

Alexander squinted his eyes. "Ah, yes, a sealing spell." He stroked his chin. "I'm afraid I never got to that chapter in class . . ."

Davi nodded, her voice calm but firm. "Sealing spells are often linked to specific words. The spell keeps the door hidden until the phrase is spoken. But here"—she gestured toward the rocks—"you're not saying it with your voice. You're speaking it by arranging the symbols in the right order."

Will raised an eyebrow. "You really are an impressive little witch."

"I used to be . . ." Davi shrugged. "Before. But that doesn't matter." She ignored the look of intrigue on Elara's face and focused her attention on the rocks.

"All right. If the spell is ultimately tied to the rocks, then we need to figure out the right order," Jasper said, picking up and turning over stones.

The group worked together to flip the stones, examining their markings. The rocks bore a variety of symbols—swirls, crescents, stars, and jagged lines. It didn't take long to realize that some stones matched symbols faintly etched around the glowing blue swirl on the mountain.

"These four," Davi said, pointing to the stones that matched the door symbols. "They're part of the phrase."

Will frowned. "All right, but what about the order? If we get it wrong, this thing might seal up tighter, or worse, blow us sky-high."

Elara's calm voice interrupted. "The symbols aren't just random shapes. They represent concepts: wind, moon, sky, and earth. The order is based on their natural relationship. Wind moves over the earth, the moon watches the sky, and everything starts with the earth itself."

Will stared at her, annoyed but impressed. "How do you know that?"

"It's written in the old tongue," Elara said, pointing to the faint inscription just beneath the blue swirl. "You don't know how to read it, do you?"

Will rolled his eyes but said nothing.

Jasper straightened, hefting one of the larger stones. "Enough talk. Let's get these into position."

Working together, the group placed the stones in a line, arranging them in the order Elara had given: earth, wind, sky, moon. As the final stone clicked into place, a low hum filled the air.

Davi stepped back, her pulse quickening. "Did it work?"

The glowing, blue swirl on the mountain blazed brighter. Then the ground beneath them began to tremble. The group stumbled as cracks spread across the rock face, radiating outward from the symbol. With a grinding sound, the wall began to part, revealing a dark, jagged opening.

A rush of cold air spilled out, carrying a faint metallic tang. Davi shivered but couldn't help the grin that spread across her face. "We did it."

Will stretched his arms, his smirk returning. "Teamwork. Told you it was my specialty."

Alexander chuckled. "Sure, Will. Right after Elara solved the puzzle for you."

Will shot him a glare but said nothing.

Davi glanced at Elara, who remained silent, her expression unreadable. There was more to her knowledge—and her past—than she let on. But now wasn't the time to press. Still, Davi couldn't ignore that Elara had proven to be valuable to them so far. First with the Wulverns and now with the puzzle.

Could Elara ever consider switching sides?

The idea seemed impossible—foolish even—but Davi couldn't stop herself from wondering. There was the Victory Clause, after all. The Games' ancient rules she'd studied had mentioned it: if the Fangslayers won, they could invite Elara to officially join their team. The clause had felt like an abstract curiosity when Davi first read it, but now . . . now it seemed like a faint glimmer of hope. Maybe Elara wasn't as bound to the Darkbane Order as she appeared. Maybe she could see her as something more than a rival.

Davi's stomach twisted with uncertainty. Trusting Elara felt dangerous, even reckless. But the idea that she might choose to stand with them—and stay—was one Davi wasn't ready to let go of.

Jasper unsheathed his sword, his face grim. "We're not done yet."

Davi nodded, her heart pounding as she stepped toward the entrance. The labyrinth waited.

15

The tunnels grew darker and more foreboding as the group descended deeper into the mountain's heart. The torches lining the walls became sparse, their flickering light barely holding back the oppressive shadows, until the light disappeared altogether. Jasper took a torch from one of the last sconces, its flame casting jagged shadows. Beside him, Alexander bound a light spell to a small pebble, which Will carried at the head of the group to illuminate their path.

Silence reigned as they moved cautiously, their senses straining for any hint of danger. Elara walked beside Davi, the two following close behind Will. Davi's hand twitched with the urge to undo Elara's bonds, but she hesitated. Alexander and Jasper were just behind them and she couldn't explain why she felt so inclined to be closer to her now.

Without warning, Elara stopped. Her body tensed like a drawn bowstring. "Stop," she whispered sharply.

"What? What is it?" Davi's voice was a strained murmur as her eyes darted around the dim tunnel.

"Zomes," Elara whispered so quietly Davi had to lean closer to catch the word. She nodded downward, her expression grim. Davi followed her gaze.

Tiny footprints dotted the dust-covered stone floor. Davi cursed herself silently for not thinking to look down, too focused on the oppressive darkness around them and Elara's proximity.

Davi motioned for the group to gather. The four closed in, their faces lit faintly by the enchanted pebble's glow.

"Zome tracks," Davi murmured, gesturing at the ground. The others' eyes followed, their expressions hardening.

"Plan?" Elara asked, her steady gaze locking onto Davi.

A flash of pride warmed Davi at being asked, but she bit her lip, her mind racing. "We usually lure them into traps with bait," she said slowly, thinking aloud.

Elara tilted her head. "That could work."

"What kind of bait?" Will interjected, his voice low but tinged with impatience. "Zomes aren't dumb creatures—they're creations of Zoli and Zola. They're clever, devious, and born to outwit. If we set a hasty trap, we'll be the ones caught."

"Right now, they have the advantage of darkness," Alexander countered, glancing at the light stone in Will's hand. "We can't fight what we can't see."

"And they'll have traps of their own set up," Jasper added. "If the Alliance placed them here, they'll be well-prepared and well-fed. Luring them out could take hours we don't have."

Will's grin was sharp in the dim light. "So, we force their hand. We flush them out and take the fight to them before they can spring anything on us."

"That's reckless," Davi shot back. "What if we walk right into their traps?"

Will tossed the light stone casually, catching it again with a smirk. "We won't if we make them show their hand first. Alexander's light spell can give us the layout of their setup."

Alexander nodded thoughtfully. "I can cast a flash spell—something bright enough to light the whole area for a few seconds. It'll ruin their night vision and give us a clear look at the terrain."

"And in those seconds, we note every trap, every hiding spot," Jasper added, his voice steady.

Davi chewed her lip but nodded. "We'll need to move quickly to keep the advantage. Alexander, after the flash spell, work on binding a light spell to a central point to maintain visibility. We'll need to keep our weapons ready to disable the traps we see before they can react. Jasper, Will, and I will engage up close while Alexander provides support from afar."

She hesitated, glancing at Elara. The newcomer's hands were still loosely bound. Davi could feel the weight of the group's silent concern pressing down on her as she spoke.

"Elara," Davi began carefully, meeting her eyes, "are you willing to fight with us?"

Elara hesitated for a fraction of a second before settling her gaze. "I am. I could have left you back there with the Wulverns," she said evenly. "Instead, I saved you. That has to count for something."

Alexander's expression darkened. "And why did you save her? You had nothing to gain."

Elara's lips curved into a faint smirk. "Nothing to gain? Hardly. If I left her and the rest of you to die, I'd be out here alone. My team's gone on without me, and there's no surviving this game alone. Keeping you alive keeps me alive."

Will crossed his arms, his voice sharp. "So, that's it? You're wanting to stick around because we're your best bet for survival?"

"Mostly," Elara admitted with a shrug, but then her tone softened, her smirk fading. "But it's not *just* that." Her eyes lingered on Davi's for a moment, her expression unreadable.

Davi's breath hitched, and for a moment, she didn't know how to respond. There was something in Elara's gaze that made her heart stumble. She tried to push it aside, to focus on the situation at hand, but the heat rising in her cheeks betrayed her.

Elara's smirk returned, sharper this time. "Believe what you want, but I need you all to survive, and I'm not stupid enough to turn on the only people who can help me get back to Gilderon now. Besides"—she glanced back at Davi, her gaze softening—"some of you are worth keeping around."

Alexander scoffed, breaking the moment. "Oh, give me a break," he murmured.

Jasper's frown deepened, but Davi ignored it. "It doesn't matter why she's here," she said, forcing her voice to stay steady despite the flutter in her chest. "What matters is that she's willing to fight with us now. That's enough."

"Is it?" Will muttered, earning a glare from Davi.

"Yes," Davi said firmly. She turned back to Elara, her fingers fumbling slightly as she untied the bindings around her wrists. "You saved me back there when you didn't have to. I believe you when you say you'll fight with us."

Elara flexed her hands as the bindings fell away, working the stiffness from her wrists. Davi unslung her bow and quiver of a dozen arrows, holding them out. "Can you use this again?"

Elara took the bow with a slow, practiced grip, testing the tension on the string. Her fingers moved with a familiarity that made it clear she knew exactly what she was doing.

"Like it's an extension of myself," she said softly, a hint of a smile playing on her lips. She slung the quiver over her shoulder, adjusting it with a wince from her injured arm.

"Cover us with long shots," Davi instructed, her voice softening despite herself. "Don't push yourself too hard—your shoulder's still—"

"I'll manage," Elara interrupted gently, her smile deepening. Her voice lowered, just enough for only Davi to hear. "Don't worry. I'm not planning on leaving your side anytime soon."

Davi's heart skipped, the words lingering longer than they should have. She tried to focus, gripping the hilts of her swords as she turned back to the group.

"Alex," she said, her voice firmer now, "prepare the flash spell. Make it fast and bright. Then find something central to bind the light to so we can keep the area visible. Once the traps are revealed, we can avoid or disable them."

Alexander nodded, his expression one of resignation.

"Let's move," Davi said, stepping into place beside Jasper. But as they began their careful advance, she couldn't help but glance back at Elara.

The archer's gaze met hers for the briefest moment, and there it was again—a flicker of something beneath the pragmatism, something that set Davi's pulse racing. She turned away quickly, her thoughts a jumble as they pressed deeper into the dark.

"Whenever you're ready, Alex," Davi called over her shoulder. She tightened her grip on her swords, scanning the darkness ahead. "Hopefully, these little buggers will be easy enough to spot," she muttered, though doubt clawed at her stomach.

Alexander raised his hand, the pebble he took from Will glowing brighter until it flared into a dazzling burst of blue witch-light. The cavern lit up around them, revealing a scene that stole Davi's breath.

The cavern stretched vast and high, a chaotic maze of jagged boulders, dangling ropes, and swaying makeshift homes attached to stalactites. The Zomes had made this place a stronghold, and their ingenuity was clear. Ropes hung low in strategic points, ready to trip or entangle, while crude spike pits lined the edges of the chamber.

And the Zomes.

Dozens of pale, wiry figures turned to face the intruders, their bulbous noses and pointed ears giving them a twisted, impish look. Their wide, sharp-toothed grins were chilling. Nearly twenty sets of gleaming eyes stared at them, and as the light faded, Davi heard the first of their high-pitched, chittering laughter.

Her stomach churned. This wasn't a handful of scavengers. This was a colony.

"Oo-whoo-hoo!" Will's whoop cut through the tension, the battle-lust clear in his voice. "It's time to prove ourselves tonight!"

"Move!" Davi roared, surging forward, her blades slicing the air. "And watch your step!"

The group sprinted into the fray, but every step brought a new hazard. Elara called out, "Tripwire ahead!" just in time for Jasper to leap over a taut line stretched between two boulders. He crashed into a Zome, shield swinging, shattering its weapon with a single blow.

Elara fired an arrow, snapping a second tripwire that released a swinging log. The log crashed harmlessly into the ground, but it sent debris flying, temporarily obscuring their vision.

"Eyes sharp!" Jasper bellowed, shielding Davi from a shower of falling rocks as they pressed forward.

Davi slashed through a rope trap that was meant to drop a net over them. "They're everywhere!" she growled, kicking aside a spiked caltrop.

"Then we destroy them!" Will yelled back, vaulting over a pit trap and flinging a dagger into the pulley mechanism of a crude, swinging blade. The blade fell uselessly to the ground, its edge dulled by rust.

The group weaved through the chaos, dodging traps and cutting down the Zomes that swarmed them. But with each second, the witch-light dimmed further, leaving them vulnerable to the dangers lurking in the shadows.

"Elara, can you clear a path?" Davi called, slashing at a Zome that lunged toward her.

Elara nocked an arrow and fired, severing another rope trap. A suspended cage crashed to the ground, crushing several Zomes beneath it. She gave Davi a grim nod, her arm trembling from the effort.

"Alex, we need that light!" Davi shouted.

"I need to get closer!" Alexander called back, dodging a crude spear hurled from above. He stumbled, nearly falling into a spike pit, but Jasper hauled him back just in time.

"This way!" Jasper bellowed, leading the charge toward a stalactite at the center of the chamber.

As the group neared the center, the Zomes' attacks grew more frantic. They darted from the shadows, chittering with glee as they triggered their own traps to slow the intruders. One Zome hurled a pouch of powder into the air, and a blinding puff of smoke erupted around them.

"Cover your mouths!" Elara warned, her voice muffled as she tied a strip of cloth over her face.

Through the haze, Alexander reached the stalactite and slammed his hand against its jagged surface. Magic surged from his fingertips as he called out a spell while covering his mouth. Light flared through the cavern once more. The blue glow illuminated the chamber, casting sharp shadows as the Zomes hissed and retreated momentarily.

"Now," Davi growled, her lips curling into a smile, "let's finish this!"

With the cavern fully illuminated, the group began to turn the tide.

Elara climbed onto a high boulder, her arrows picking off Zomes from above. Spotting a rope trap near a cluster of Zomes, she fired a shot that triggered it. The rope snapped, releasing a boulder that tumbled down and scattered the creatures.

Davi and Jasper worked in tandem, dismantling traps as they fought. Jasper's sword crushed a spring-loaded mechanism, while Davi used her swords to cut through a snare before it could catch Will's leg.

"Use their tricks against them!" Davi yelled, her swords flashing as she fought her way toward Elara.

Just as victory seemed within reach, a Zome lashed a rope around Elara's legs and yanked her from her perch. She crashed to the ground, her bow skittering out of reach.

"Elara!" Davi screamed, her heart pounding as she watched the archer struggle against the rope. A group of Zomes closed in, their sharp teeth bared.

Davi surged forward, slashing wildly at the creatures in her path. Pain flared in her side as a Zome's claw raked across her armor, but she didn't slow.

Jasper called out, "Davi, fall back! You'll be killed!"

But she ignored him, her focus entirely on Elara.

Her blade wasn't enough. She knew it as she watched the sheer number of Zomes swarming toward Elara. Panic seized her chest as her thoughts leapt to the one thing she had tried so hard to avoid. Her magic.

Davi reached for it easily and that realization hit her even as the raw energy surged through her, like it had been waiting for her to finally give in.

What am I doing? she thought, even as her hand rose toward the Zomes. This was never her answer. Why was she so willing to use it now? But she needed to. Elara wouldn't survive this if she didn't.

The spell exploded outward, a shockwave of energy that threw the creatures back. The force shattered the ground beneath them, cracks spidering outward as the cavern floor began to collapse.

"No!" Davi shouted, her voice breaking as she dove toward Elara.

Elara locked eyes with Davi, her hand outstretched, just as the ground beneath them gave way. They fell into the darkness together, the chaos of the battle fading into a deafening silence.

16

They hit the ground hard, the impact reverberating through Davi's body like a punch to the chest. Rocks and dirt exploded into the air, the acrid dust stinging her throat and filling her lungs as she coughed violently. Instinctively, she curled into a ball, covering her head as debris rained down around her like a relentless thunderstorm.

Finally, the chaos ceased. Silence settled, broken only by the faint rustle of dirt sliding down the pit walls. Davi slowly lifted her head, her heart pounding in her ears. "Elara?" she called, her voice tight with worry, slicing through the stillness.

A ragged cough answered her. Relief surged through Davi as she scrambled toward the sound, her hands fumbling in the darkness until they found warm skin. "Elara! Are you okay? Say something—please."

Elara coughed again, the sound sharp and raw, as she moved under Davi's touch. Rocks slid and shifted as she began to push herself upright. The haze of dust finally began to settle, and faint light from Alex's spell above filtered into the pit, casting dim, ghostly shadows over the jagged walls.

"I'm fine," Elara rasped, her voice strained but steady.

Relief gave way to guilt. "I'm so sorry," Davi said, the words spilling out in a rush. "I didn't mean for that to happen—I didn't—"

As her eyes adjusted to the dim light, Davi saw Elara's face—and her stomach twisted. Fear clouded her expression, her bright green eyes wide and uncertain. Beneath it, Davi caught something else: hesitation. Fear.

Elara didn't meet her gaze right away. "Your power," she began, her voice faltering before sharpening with an edge of accusation. "It's more powerful than anything I've ever seen."

Davi's breath hitched. She opened her mouth to reply, but the words stuck in her throat. There was no excuse this time. Her magic had obeyed her, but she'd been reckless—again. Just like in the arena, when Alex was in danger. She'd acted too quickly, and now . . . now Elara looked at her like everyone else did when they found out the truth.

Like something monstrous.

The silence between them stretched, heavy and suffocating. Davi could feel Elara's judgmental gaze, and she wanted to shrink away from it. Her magic had betrayed her again, and now that was all Elara would see. That was all anyone ever saw—everyone except Alex and Jasper. Tears prickled at the corners of Davi's eyes, but she blinked them back. The fragile bond she'd been building with Elara was gone, shattered in an instant.

"Thanks for saving me," Elara said, breaking the silence. Her voice was softer now, almost sad. "I guess that makes us even."

"I hardly saved you," Davi replied flatly, standing and brushing the dust from her clothes. Her voice was distant, hollow. "We're stuck in this pit now."

"Can you use your magic?" Elara asked, tucking her necklace into her shirt and looking up toward the opening. Her tone was light, hopeful even, but Davi stiffened at the suggestion. "You could lift us out, or create a ladder with the rock, or maybe even make a portal to the top?"

Davi flinched. There was a tentative smile on Elara's face, but her eyes were bright with expectation. Not admiration—expectation.

"No," Davi said sharply, her voice clipped.

Elara blinked in surprise. "What? Why not? I know you can do extraordinary things. I saw you in the arena—how you pushed me away from Alexander with wind, and then the power you wielded in the woods—"

"I said no!" Davi snapped, her voice cracking like a whip.

Elara stepped back slightly, raising her hands as if to calm her. "Why won't you own your power?" she asked softly. Her tone shifted, no longer accusing but probing, vulnerable. "Why are you hiding yourself? Not just your power, but who you are. You act tough, like you don't care, but I've seen you. I've seen how fiercely you protect the people you care about."

Davi's breath hitched. The words struck too close to home, and anger flared in her chest, hot and defensive. She forced it down, clamping her arms across her chest. "I don't hide anything," she muttered, her voice low. "I'm just a better fighter than a witch. That's all. You don't know me at all. Alex is the real witch on the team. He's much better than I am."

"That's not true," Elara said firmly, her voice rising. "You're more than talented, Davi. You have innate power. It's unlike anything—"

"Enough." Davi shook her off, her voice cold with finality. Who was Elara to push her like this? To pry open wounds she'd worked so hard to seal? Without another word, she turned and strode to the center of the cavern, where the faint light from above mocked her with its distance.

Elara followed, her voice quiet but insistent. "Why won't you just embrace your magic? Maybe it would be easier if—"

Davi rounded on her, her anger flaring hot and unrestrained. "You have no idea what magic is," she bit out. "You have no idea what it does to me. My magic is dangerous. It's—torturous."

A sharp, stabbing ache flared in her arm, making her stagger. She clutched at it instinctively, but Elara was already there, catching her hand to steady her. Their eyes met, and for a moment, Davi saw something she dreaded more than anything else: pity.

She wrenched her hand away, her voice raw and shaking. "When I use my magic, it's like I'm being ripped apart—physically, mentally. It *hurts*. Every time I use it, it's like burning alive from the inside out. And every time, I remember why I need to stop."

Elara's face softened, but Davi turned away before she could say anything. She didn't want comfort. She didn't want understanding. She wanted to be free. Free of her power, free of her past, free of the endless weight of being something no one could truly accept. Not even Elara.

"Magic shouldn't feel that way," Elara mumbled, her voice soft but certain. "Someone hurt you, didn't they?" The question came quietly, carefully, her tone betraying both compassion and trepidation.

Davi stiffened, her mind racing. *How does she know what magic should feel like?* The thought stirred a rush of anger in her, sharp and defensive, but just as quickly, something else followed—a release. It wasn't the release of rage or indignation. It was something sweeter. Tears welled up and began to spill, unstoppable, streaking her dust-covered face.

Jasper had always been there during her panic attacks, grounding her with his steady presence. Alexander had been the one to see what the others in the village hadn't, whisking them both away before it was too late. But no one had ever asked her this. No one had asked what was wrong—not truly. They didn't want to know, didn't want to touch the truth. And Davi had been content to let it stay buried.

But now? Maybe it was time to stop hiding. She felt a comfort with Elara that she couldn't explain.

"You said your magic tortures you," Elara said, her voice gentle but insistent. "It's okay if you don't want to talk about it. But . . . if you do, I'm here. You can tell me. I'll listen."

Davi bit her lip hard, the metallic tang of blood filling her mouth as she tore at the fragile skin. The tears kept coming, and her breaths hitched in uneven gasps. She didn't want to speak, but the words clawed at her, begging to be let out.

Elara moved closer, her hand hovering just shy of Davi's arm before resting there, light but steady. It was the same way Davi had felt when Elara touched her back at camp, a silent offering of comfort.

Elara's touch was warm, grounding. Her eyes—earnest, open—met Davi's. And in that moment, Davi felt safe. She felt seen.

The words broke free before she could stop them.

"My teacher," Davi began, her voice barely a whisper. "He took a liking to me."

Elara said nothing, her expression soft but intent, urging her to continue.

"It was flattering at first," Davi admitted, her gaze fixed on the dirt. "I was the most talented witch in the village, the most powerful. But he . . . he was the one with the real power. He had everyone's trust—the hearts of the entire village. He was the highest-ranking witch in Raventon. He didn't just teach us; he made us. Literally. He performed the blood rituals on all the babies. It was his blood that made us witches."

Elara's brow furrowed, her lips parting as if to speak, but she held back.

Davi's voice faltered, but she pressed on, her words tumbling out in a rush. "I don't know if it was something in his blood or the way he performed the rituals, but he only lost two babies to the darkness in all his years. That's rare. Usually, more don't survive. The ones who don't make it . . . they become demons and have to be put to death. But because of him, so many of us lived."

She paused, the weight of what she was about to say catching in her throat. "But he thought that meant he owned us. Especially me."

Elara's hand tightened slightly on her arm, a small but firm reminder that she wasn't alone.

"At first, it was just . . . comments. Lingering touches. Things I could ignore." Davi's voice cracked, and she buried her face in her hands. "But eventually . . ."

She couldn't finish. She didn't need to.

Elara moved closer, wrapping her arms around Davi in a firm embrace. "It's not your fault," she whispered, her voice fierce despite its softness. "You did nothing wrong."

The words shattered the dam inside Davi, and the floodgates opened. Sobs racked her body, the emotions she'd buried for so long tearing free in waves. "I shouldn't have said—" she gasped, the words choked out between breaths. "I've never told—"

"It's all right," Elara assured her, pulling back just enough to meet Davi's eyes. "I'm glad you did."

For a long moment, they sat in the quiet, broken only by Davi's uneven breaths. Finally, Elara spoke again, her tone laced with a rare vulnerability. "When my village was ransacked by raiders, I became a slave. My time in captivity was . . . it was filled with men like your teacher." Her lips pressed into a thin line. "But I didn't know them. I didn't love them. It made it easier to hate them. Easier to manipulate them."

Her voice turned bitter, laced with something darker. "That's how I survived. I used what they wanted from me to get what I needed. It's how I escaped. It's how I made my way to the city. And even then, the only place for someone like me was a brothel." She gave a humorless laugh. "I told myself it was my choice, but deep down . . . I don't know if it ever really was."

Elara reached out, brushing a tear from Davi's cheek. "If I had known those men, if I had cared for them or respected them even a little . . . I don't think I would've made it out. You're stronger than you think, Davi. What you did? Coming here? That took courage."

Davi shook her head, her lips trembling. "It wasn't brave. It's what we're supposed to do. All the talented witches in my village leave when we're ready. We find contracts with nobles, send money back home. It's just . . . tradition."

"It's always brave to take your fate into your own hands," Elara said softly.

Davi hesitated, then admitted, "I tried to work for the Morningfires, actually."

Elara's eyes widened. "The Morningfires? Charles's Morningfires?"

"I never did though," Davi said quickly. "I saw him touch a maid in a way that made me uncomfortable, but it wasn't just that." She hesitated, unsure how much to reveal, but Elara's expression was so open, so inviting. Davi relented. "I wasn't sure I could use my magic reliably. My disease won't let me. Not without the potions from home. And I refuse to take them. I can't . . . not when I know who is making them. So, I left the Morningfire interview before it truly started."

Elara frowned, her gaze sharpening with concern. "Your disease?"

Davi nodded, exhaling shakily. She tugged at her armor, exposing her shoulder and upper chest. Dark, jagged lines traced her skin, faintly pulsing as if alive.

Elara's fingers brushed the lines gently, and Davi shivered at the contact. The lines flared faintly under her touch, reacting as though recognizing her. For a fleeting moment, Davi relished the warmth, the connection. But it was too much. Too dangerous. She pulled away, covering herself again.

"Do they hurt?" Elara asked, her voice quiet.

Davi laughed bitterly. "Sometimes. It's sneaky, though. Most of the time, it's just nausea. Intermittent pain. But it's always there, waiting."

Elara's gaze turned thoughtful. "The Healing Stone could help you too," she murmured, almost to herself.

Davi's ears perked up. "The Healing Stone?" she asked, her curiosity sharpening. "The Lumos Gem?"

Elara nodded. "Yes. Charles swears we can find it if we get into the Alliance."

Davi frowned, skepticism etched across her face. "You trust him?"

Elara let out a dry laugh, shaking her head. "No, of course not. Trusting Charles is like trusting a snake not to bite you. But—" her voice softened, her gaze distant—"he found me in the brothel, and for whatever reason, he saw something in me worth saving. At least, that's what he likes to say."

"Why would he do that?" Davi asked, her suspicion deepening. "What does he get out of it?"

Elara's lips pressed into a tight line, her voice edged with bitterness. "Charles always has his reasons. He doesn't care about me, not really. He wants the Healing Stone for his own glory. He thinks if he gets us into the Alliance and finds the Stone, he'll be a hero—someone his father can finally be proud of. He dreams of resurrecting the Lumos Gems Hunts, making them legendary again. It's not about the Alliance or the Stone; it's about him."

Davi studied Elara's face, her unease growing. "But why do you need it?" she asked, the question barely a whisper. Fear curled in her stomach, bracing for an answer she wasn't sure she wanted to hear.

Elara hesitated, her expression heavy with emotion. Then, with deliberate slowness, she unfastened the top of her tunic, revealing a mark over her heart. It shimmered faintly, a dark, intricate spiral of dots, like ink bleeding through her skin.

Davi stared, her breath catching in her throat. "What . . . what is that?" She reached out instinctively, her fingers trembling.

Elara caught her hand, guiding it to the mark. The warmth of her skin beneath Davi's fingers was startling, and for a moment, the world around them seemed to fall away.

"It's a curse," Elara said quietly. "One that has no cure. Not unless we find the Healing Stone."

Davi's heart clenched. Her voice was barely steady as she replied, "Then forget Charles. Forget the Alliance. We could find the Healing Stone ourselves. Together."

Elara's eyes met hers, wide and glistening with unshed tears. She looked at Davi as if she'd just offered her a lifeline, a spark of hope in the darkness. For a moment, neither of them spoke, the weight of their unspoken emotions filling the air.

Then Davi moved, her body acting before her mind could catch up. She leaned in, her lips brushing Elara's in a kiss that was as much a confession as it was an act of longing. The kiss was passionate, hungry, their shared pain and vulnerability igniting like a flame between them.

For the first time in so long, Davi felt alive—truly alive. The world around them dissolved, and all that existed was the warmth of Elara's touch, the press of her lips, the way her hand cupped Davi's cheek so tenderly it almost broke her. She never wanted the moment to end.

But it did.

"Davi!" Alexander's voice echoed down the cavern, sharp and insistent.

The sound jolted her back to the present. She froze, her breath hitching as the weight of everything—Elara's mysterious curse, the kiss, the questions—settled heavy in her chest.

"Davi, are you down there?" Alexander called again, closer now. "Answer me!"

"I'm here!" Davi shouted back, her voice strong, cutting through the tension. "We're all right!"

Moments later, a rope dropped into the pit, its frayed ends swaying faintly. Without a word, Elara reached for it, her movements swift but tense, as if she was trying to mask the emotions simmering beneath the surface.

The men pulled them up out of the pit, and when they reached the top, Alexander, Jasper, and Will met them with strained breaths. Alexander's relief was palpable as he pulled Davi in for a hug. "I thought we'd lost you."

Before Davi could respond, Alexander pushed her away and took something from his belt—a circular piece of intricately designed metal that gleamed faintly in the blue light still surrounding them. The pattern was mesmerizing, etched with ancient symbols and sharp, deliberate lines that formed a spiral at its center.

Davi's heart leapt. "Is that—?"

"The first piece," Alexander confirmed, holding it up for her to see.

She snatched it from him, her fingers trembling as she turned it over. The craftsmanship was extraordinary. "Where did you find it?"

"One of the Zomes' traps," he said, brushing dirt from his hands. "Will spotted it while we were looking for you."

Davi clutched the piece tightly, the weight of it grounding her for a moment. They were close. So close. Just one more piece, and they'd be able to open the dragon's lair.

"We need to move," she said suddenly, urgency flooding her voice. "If the Darkbane Order gets to the gate before we do . . ."

"They won't," Jasper said, but his expression betrayed a flicker of doubt.

"They can't," Davi insisted, slipping the piece into her bag and tightening the strap. "We'll find the last piece quickly. We have to."

Elara's gaze lingered on Davi for a moment, her face unreadable, but she said nothing. Davi turned away, ignoring the warmth still lingering from the kiss and the burning sensation of the desire she'd felt.

Davi gestured toward the path ahead. "Let's move out. Jasper, lead the way."

Jasper nodded and pulled a torch from the wall to lead them through the darkness of the caverns ahead. As they started down the winding trail, the key's weight in her bag seemed to push Davi forward, her steps fueled by determination. One piece left. One chance to claim the lair.

And for the first time in a long time, Davi felt like she wasn't just running from her past. Her chosen destiny was within her grasp.

17

As the group began to move, Davi could feel Elara's gaze on her, a silent weight that pressed against her back like the promise of an unfinished conversation. Unspoken words hung between them, fragile and trembling, but Davi didn't dare turn around. Not yet. Not until she could steady the emotions threatening to pull her under.

Her eyes dropped to her boots as they shuffled one step after another, the rhythm doing little to quiet her thoughts. She couldn't shake the memory of the kiss, the longing that had consumed her in the pit. It was ridiculous, overwhelming, and utterly inescapable. How could she feel so willing to reshape her life for someone she barely knew? She had poured out her soul to her so easily. She told her things she'd never told anyone. And it had all felt so easy and comfortable. Jasper had always been grounding and steady for her, but Elara made her feel truly seen.

Lost in thought, she bumped into Jasper's broad back. "Oh, sorry," she mumbled, blinking as she realized the group had stopped. "Why did we stop?"

Jasper pointed ahead. The stone path ended abruptly, giving way to a vast expanse of dark water that stretched into the shadows. Torches lined the cavern walls, their flickering light reflecting in rippling patterns across the surface.

At the water's edge, tied to a single wooden pole, was a small boat—worn, rickety, and entirely out of place.

Will was already striding toward it, his boots crunching on loose pebbles. He stopped a few paces away, rubbing his chin as he surveyed it with a skeptical frown. "Hmmm," he mused aloud, turning to look at the group. "So . . . who's staying behind?"

Davi's jaw tightened. "What are you talking about?"

Will gestured to the boat. "This thing barely fits four people, and there are five of us. It's simple math. Someone's got to stay, and, well . . ." He tilted his head toward Elara.

Elara stiffened but said nothing, her expression guarded.

Davi stepped forward, her voice cold and sharp. "She's coming with us."

Will raised his hands, mock surrender in his stance. "Look, I get it, she helped us back there. Great. But she's not part of the team. She's already done more than enough to repay the favor—"

"I said no," Davi snapped, her glare piercing.

Will hesitated, glancing at Jasper for support. "Come on, big guy, back me up here. It's a tiny boat."

Jasper paused, his gaze flicking between Davi and Elara. The tension was thick, but when Davi's eyes locked on his, the answer was clear. "We're not leaving anyone behind," he said firmly, stepping past Will and climbing into the boat.

Will groaned, throwing his hands up. "Fine. But when we all end up in the water because this thing capsizes, don't say I didn't warn you."

Alexander eyed the boat warily. "He's not wrong about the size. This thing was definitely made for four, not five."

"We'll figure it out," Jasper grunted, adjusting his weight to test the boat's balance.

Davi's voice cut through the discussion like steel. "Get in."

One by one, the others complied. Will muttered something under his breath but stepped in grudgingly, while Alexander cast a worried glance back at the cavern. Elara lingered, her eyes meeting Davi's briefly before she followed the others.

Davi was the last to board, her gaze scanning the cavern walls and the eerily still water. The torches ahead stretched into the distance, their reflections wavering like spectral flames. The air felt heavy, as if something unseen was watching, waiting.

This wasn't just another obstacle. The Zomes and Wulverns they'd faced earlier were trials, yes, but this? This was a threshold. Whatever lay ahead was different. Worse.

Davi settled into the boat, her hand brushing the hilt of her blade. "Row," she said, her voice low but resolute.

Jasper took the oars, the boat creaking as it drifted forward.

The boat rocked under their weight as it glided through the cavern's dimly lit waters. Everyone was on edge, their silence laden with the anticipation of danger.

Elara winced, clutching her chest. Davi opened her mouth to ask if she was all right, but Alexander's hand gripped her arm suddenly.

"What's that?" he asked, pointing ahead.

Davi squinted into the gloom. On a large rock near the water's edge lay a figure—a girl, her black hair cascading over her face, her small body sprawled in an unnatural stillness.

"We should sail past," Will said, his voice clipped.

"We can't just leave her there," Alexander countered, concern rising in his tone. "She's clearly in trouble!"

"We don't know her, and we can't afford to slow down," Will argued. "It's probably a trap."

"Or she might know something—about the dragon, about the Order," Alexander reasoned, his voice tight with urgency.

Davi's gaze lingered on the girl as they drew closer. She looked so fragile, so helpless. Was she a sacrifice left for the dragon? A victim of this treacherous cavern? The thought made Davi's stomach twist.

"Jasper," Alexander said, his voice desperate now, "we can't just leave her. Please. We need to make sure she's all right."

Jasper glanced at Alexander, then to Davi. His hesitation was brief, but Davi knew he wouldn't abandon someone, not like this. She gave him a slight nod, and he returned it grimly.

Will threw up his hands. "This is insane. It's obviously a trap! But fine—let's waste time saving the obvious bait!"

"Hold us steady," Jasper commanded as he guided the boat to the rock. He gripped the stone with one hand while Will begrudgingly leaned out to anchor them.

"Stay here," Davi whispered to Elara before stepping onto the rock with Jasper and Alexander and drawing a sword.

Alexander crouched beside the girl and brushed her hair back from her face. Davi sucked in a breath. The girl was breathtakingly beautiful—too beautiful. Her skin was flawless, her delicate features perfectly sculpted, and even in unconscious stillness, she radiated an unnatural allure.

The girl's eyes fluttered open, revealing a vivid blue gaze that locked onto Alexander with startling intensity. She smiled—a slow, knowing smile that sent a chill crawling down Davi's spine.

"Alex, no!" Davi hissed, reaching for her brother, but it was too late.

The girl's hand darted out, wrapping around Alexander's arm. His body froze in place, his eyes wide and glassy. Slowly, the girl sat up, her long hair falling around her like a dark veil, her movements graceful and predatory.

Davi grabbed Alexander's shoulder and pulled with all her strength, but he resisted, leaning closer to the girl. She coiled herself around him, her lips nearing his.

"Jasper! Help me!" Davi shouted, panic surging in her chest.

Jasper, however, stood motionless, his face slack and dreamy as he stared at the girl.

"She's a Demona!" Davi yelled. "We have to get away from her now!"

"Oh, great!" Will's voice called from the boat. "I told you this was a trap!"

Desperation clawed at Davi as she turned to Jasper. She grabbed his shoulders, shaking him violently. "Jasper, snap out of it! Don't let them win!" Her voice broke as tears streamed down her cheeks.

"Davi"—Elara's voice came from the boat, sharp and urgent—"she's not the only one. We're surrounded."

Davi's heart sank. She turned back to Alexander, whose lips were inches from the Demona's. If she kissed him, his life force would drain away in moments.

"Jasper, please!" Davi begged, her voice a desperate whisper. "Remember the moonlight!"

At those words, Jasper blinked, his eyes clearing. The light returned to them, and Davi sobbed in relief. Jasper's expression hardened, and he grabbed Alexander by the collar, yanking him back with all his might.

The Demona shrieked, her nails raking across Alexander's arm as she tried to keep hold. Jasper pulled harder, his muscles straining, until Alexander came free. Davi delivered a fierce kick to the creature's chest, sending her sliding off the rock and plunging into the dark water with a piercing wail.

Jasper hoisted Alexander over his shoulder, and the three scrambled back toward the boat as shadows moved in the periphery.

"Row! Now!" Davi shouted as they leapt into the boat.

Will didn't need to be told twice. The oars dipped into the water, propelling them forward as inhuman cries echoed through the cavern behind them. Davi clutched Alexander, whose dazed expression slowly gave way to confusion, then terror.

"What—what happened?" he stammered.

"You're an idiot, that's what happened," Davi said, her voice shaking as she glanced over her shoulder.

Davi's breath hitched as she looked ahead. The horizon was teeming with otherworldly beauty. Demonas of all kinds encircled them, their radiant forms a mesmerizing menace. Some resembled Aurens, their wings of purest white or darkest black spreading like celestial tapestries, shimmering in the dim light. Others emerged sinuously from the water, like Rivens with hair like flowing rainbows and skin that glittered like wet jewels.

Their voices wove a seductive spell, soft and sweet, promising rest, safety, and care.

"We need to restrain him," Davi barked, her own voice strained as she fought the pull of their call. Together with Jasper, she bound Alexander, who thrashed against the ropes, his eyes glassy with longing.

"Me too . . . better tie me too . . ." Will slurred, his hand drifting toward the nearest Riven Demona who was watching him with a playful smile.

"Damn it, Will!" Davi hissed, grabbing him before he could lurch toward the water. She wrestled him back, quickly looping the rope around his chest as Jasper tightened Alexander's bindings.

And then, through the chaos, a voice rose.

Elara was singing.

The sound silenced the cavern, a melody steeped in yearning and sorrow, as though it had been birthed from the deepest recesses of the heart. Davi's muscles slackened, the tension in her chest unraveling with each note. The words were foreign, but their meaning transcended language. This was a song of love, of grief, of hope too fragile to name.

Elara sang with her eyes closed, her head tilted back as if the music was drawn from the heavens themselves. Her voice seemed to ripple through the air, disrupting the unnatural pull of the Demonas' luring song.

Davi glanced at the others. The ropes no longer strained against Alexander and Will; their struggles had ceased, their breathing slowed. Jasper's shoulders, once knotted with tension, had eased. Even the Demonas paused, their voices momentarily quieted, their perfect faces tilting in faint wonder at why their song wasn't working.

The Demona voices rose again, stronger this time, but still they didn't attack. Davi had read that they never strike first unless provoked. Their power lay not in brute force but in their song: an alluring web that drew prey closer, helpless to resist until they could reach out and drain the life from their victims. They wanted their prey alive and willing, close enough to touch.

Elara's voice was doing something, creating a countermelody that cut through the Demonas' magic. *How did she know exactly how to do that?* Davi wondered, but didn't dare to disrupt her now.

The boat drifted slowly through the narrowing chasm, the air thick with the haunting melodies of the Demonas. Davi's gaze swept over the creatures, marveling at their beauty and restraint. They still did not advance, only watched and sang, their allure almost tangible, though their piercing gazes hinted at hunger.

Her eyes flicked to the archway ahead, its jagged stone promising an escape. Relief stirred faintly in her chest—until she saw her.

Next to the arch sat a Demona unlike the others, enthroned on a dais of black stone. Her scarlet wings fanned out behind her, their shimmering hue catching the flickering torchlight. A black necklace gleamed around her neck, a swirling piece of dark metal dangling at its center. It twisted and curved in an intricate pattern, its shape resembling the jagged teeth of a key. Their last piece.

Davi's heart clenched. *Of course.*

The Demona rose, her crimson eyes locking onto Davi's. Her lips parted, and her voice poured forth, rich and honeyed, sliding beneath Davi's skin like liquid fire.

"Stop the boat," Davi said, her voice low but firm.

Jasper stiffened at the oars. "What? No way. We're almost through!"

"We need the last piece of the key. And she has it," Davi said, nodding toward the scarlet-winged creature.

"She's stronger than the others," Elara murmured from the stern, her voice raw from singing. Sweat glistened on her brow.

"I'll be quick," Davi said firmly, throwing off her boots and removing her armor.

Jasper's hands tightened on the oars, his jaw clenching. "You can't fight her alone."

"I'm not fighting her," Davi said, standing in her underclothes. Her legs felt like lead, but her voice held steady. "They'll all attack if I strike first. I'll get the key without violence."

Davi turned to Elara, their eyes meeting. "If I don't make it back . . . Get them out of here."

Elara's expression twisted, but she gave a sharp nod. "Don't kill any of them," she warned. "My song won't reach you out there. You have to resist her."

Davi nodded. Her mouth was dry, her heart pounding against her ribs, but she forced herself to dive into the water.

"Davi, don't—" Jasper started, but she was already moving.

The icy shock stole her breath, but she pushed forward, her strokes steady as the Demonas' eyes followed her every move.

The Riven Demonas in the water swam closer, their lithe bodies slicing through the depths like predators. Their hands reached toward her, but she didn't stop, didn't look. Her focus was on the throne and the scarlet-winged creature watching her with a knowing smile.

The Demona stood as Davi climbed onto the dais, water streaming from her clothes. Up close, her beauty was devastating, her crimson hair flowing like molten fire, her features perfect and unearthly.

"You want this?" the Demona asked, her voice wrapping around Davi like silk as she gestured to the necklace.

"Yes," Davi said, her voice cracking. "I need it."

The Demona smiled, stepping closer. "And what will you give me for it, dear one?" Her hands grazed Davi's arms, her touch light as a whisper. "You're strong to resist my sisters, but I see your heart. I see what you crave."

Davi froze as the Demona's fingers traced her cheek.

"You want to be loved," the Demona murmured, her voice a balm that soothed and stung. "To be held. To be seen."

Tears stung Davi's eyes, unbidden.

"Come," the Demona whispered, pulling her into an embrace. "I can give you all that. Stay with me, and you will never want for anything again."

For a moment, Davi faltered. Her body ached for the comfort offered, her heart screaming for the warmth she'd always been denied. The Demona's arms tightened around her, and her voice became a low, soothing hum, pulling Davi closer to the edge of surrender.

But then Davi's eyes fell on the necklace.

She clenched her jaw, her fists curling at her sides. With a swift, practiced motion, she reached up and ripped the necklace from the Demona's neck.

The Demona shrieked, the sound splitting the air as Davi turned and dove back into the water, the key clutched tightly in her hand.

The water exploded around her as the Demonas surged after her, their hands clawing at her legs and pulling her down. She kicked fiercely, her lungs burning as she fought to stay afloat.

"Davi!" Jasper's voice roared above the chaos.

She broke the surface, gasping for air, her hand shooting up toward the boat. Jasper grabbed her wrist, yanking her out of the water just as a Demona lunged for her ankles.

She collapsed onto the boat's floor, coughing and sputtering, the necklace still clutched tightly in her fist.

"Row!" Jasper bellowed, shoving off the rock as Elara scrambled to row.

The boat surged forward, the Demonas hissing and shrieking behind them, their wings beating the air and claws slicing the water, but they didn't give chase.

Davi looked down at the key in her hand, her breath ragged but steady.

"Got it," she murmured, her voice trembling.

Jasper knelt beside her, his eyes blazing with relief and fury. "Don't ever do that again."

Davi leaned back against the boat's edge, her heart still pounding.

She dared to look back at the Demonas. Their beauty was a kaleidoscope of elegance that should have stolen her breath. They called out still, their voices softening into a chant that thrummed with impossible allure.

But Davi felt nothing.

18

The boat scraped against rocks, jolting them to a halt. Elara's song had tapered off, leaving a heavy silence in its wake. The boys stopped struggling against their restraints, the trance of the Demonas finally broken.

Davi scanned their surroundings. The narrow archway had given way to a labyrinth of dark corridors, their jagged walls glistening faintly with moisture. They'd made it.

A collective sigh of relief swept through the boat. Jasper dropped the oars and rolled his shoulders, wincing.

"Oh, thank the gods," Alexander groaned, lying flat on his back to stare at the cavern ceiling. "Sorry about that, folks. My bad . . ."

"You didn't know," Davi said, her voice steady.

"Well," Will cut in, arching a brow, "*I* had a feeling."

"It doesn't matter now," Jasper said, wiping sweat from his brow. "We had no choice but to face them." His gaze flicked to Davi before darting away, his expression unreadable. "It's better that we knew what we were dealing with before rowing into the masses of them."

Davi's cheeks warmed as she fumbled to explain what happened. "Elara's song . . . It somehow countered their alluring spell."

"Countered them?" Alexander pressed, his sharp eyes narrowing. "How did you know to sing in the first place? And how did it work? Was it just luck?"

Elara's expression flickered, her usual composure slipping for just a moment. She met Alexander's gaze with a measured calm, though her fingers fidgeted in her lap. "It wasn't luck," she said softly. "The right song can create interference—enough to break through their influence. It doesn't defeat them, but it buys time."

"How do you even know that?" Will asked, his tone tinged with suspicion. "Most people don't walk around with a manual for dealing with Demonas."

Elara hesitated, glancing at Davi for a fleeting second before answering. "I've had . . . experience with them before." Her voice was steady, but something about the way she said it made Davi's chest tighten. "I've had experience with all the monsters we've faced."

Davi watched her carefully, noting the tightness in her jaw, the way her shoulders seemed slightly stiff, and she couldn't help the feeling that there was far more to Elara's story than she was sharing. And as much as she wanted to push for answers, she also knew it was better to let people share their stories when they were ready.

"That's grand and all," Alexander interrupted, struggling against his restraints. "Now, can someone please untie us?"

Relieved for the excuse to drop the subject, Davi nodded. She, Jasper, and Elara worked quickly to undo the ropes. Once freed, the group climbed out of the boat, their boots crunching against the cavern floor.

"We need to assemble the key now," Elara said, her calm tone carrying a quiet authority. The word "we" sent an unexpected flutter through Davi's chest.

Alexander gave Elara a sidelong glance but said nothing as he pulled the other piece of the key from his bag. Snapping the two halves together with a satisfying click, he held up the now-complete key.

"We did it," Davi whispered, a flicker of awe in her voice.

Will snorted. "Don't get too smug yet. We've still got the hardest part ahead of us. You know, the dragon."

The weight of the reminder settled over them like a heavy fog. Davi nodded grimly. "You're right. Let's take a moment to regroup. Alexander, review your spells. Everyone, eat something while you can."

She dropped her pack and rummaged through it, handing out small rations and potions. She found a chain and strung the key onto it before placing it around her neck and tucking it into her shirt, wanting to keep it safe. The group ate in silence, the tension thick in the air. When they were ready, Davi stood and gestured toward the darkness ahead.

"Let's finish this," she said, gripping her torch tightly.

They moved forward, their footsteps echoing on the stone floor. The tunnel narrowed before them, the faint glimmer of light ahead casting their long shadows on the walls. Davi's heart pounded faster with every step, a mix of dread and resolve churning in her chest.

Will suddenly stopped, his arm shooting out to block their path.

"What is it?" Davi whispered, her stomach knotting.

"Look up there," Will said, nodding toward the tunnel's end.

Davi squinted but could only make out a bright, silvery glow. "What am I supposed to be seeing?"

"Giants," Will said, his voice heavy with irritation as he turned to glare at her.

"Giants?" Alexander groaned, throwing his head back in exasperation.

"We should've seen that coming," Jasper muttered, running a hand through his dirty blond hair.

Davi exhaled slowly. "Yeah. I guess we should have. Besides Xevrals, they're the only type of Elusiran monster we haven't faced." She stepped closer, her eyes narrowing as she studied the shapes ahead. "How many?"

Will edged forward, peering into the light. "Two . . . that I can see. Big brutes with spiked clubs."

The tension among the group was palpable. Davi gritted her teeth and glanced back at the others.

"But if the giants are still here, it means the Darkbane Order hasn't been through yet," Jasper said, his voice low but urgent.

"Does it?" Will asked skeptically.

"Yeah," Jasper nodded toward the scene ahead. "Look what they're guarding."

Behind the towering giants loomed a massive iron gate, its surface gleaming faintly in the fading sunlight that filtered through the cavern. The final gate. Still locked, still untouched. They weren't too late. Relief washed over Davi, but it was fleeting.

"We need to handle this efficiently," Davi said, her tone sharpening as she addressed the group. "We can't waste too much energy before the dragon fight. Keep your distance, use the environment, and remember, we work as a team. No one runs ahead. No one gets left behind. We spread out when I give the call."

The group nodded, but Davi's gaze lingered on Elara, doubt flickering like a shadow at the edge of her thoughts. She wasn't the only one wondering—would Elara fight with them again? Could they trust her, *truly* trust her?

Elara, catching the unspoken question in their eyes, reached for the edge of her bandage. Slowly, deliberately, she unwound it, revealing the pale scars etched into her skin like ancient runes. They caught the faint light, a testament to battles fought and survived.

She looked up and smiled, her expression calm and unwavering. "I'm with you," she said softly, placing a steadying hand on Davi's shoulder. "This will be fun."

Davi's chest tightened, a strange warmth blooming despite the tension. She nodded, forcing her face into neutral composure even as the corner of her lips twitched upward.

She turned to the others. Will's eyes narrowed slightly, flicking between Elara's and her face, but after a beat, he gave a sharp nod. "She's helped us so far. Might as well see it through."

Jasper exhaled through his nose, his lips pressing into a thin line. "She's given me no reason to distrust her word."

Alexander, still rubbing his wrists from the earlier restraints, shot Elara a playful grin. "As long as she doesn't start singing like those Demonas, I'm good."

Elara's smile widened, her eyes glinting with humor, but she didn't respond. She glanced at Davi instead, her trust evident in the quiet connection between them.

Davi drew in a steadying breath, her voice firm and brisk as she addressed the group. "All right. Let's get past these buffoons."

They turned toward the giants. The hulking figures shifted their massive forms, sensing the challenge before them. Spiked clubs scraped against the rocky ground, the sound grating and ominous.

Weapons were drawn, the faint rasp of steel echoing in the heavy air. Davi gripped her sword tighter, her pulse quickening.

For a moment, there was silence. Just the empty clearing, the giants, and the faint rhythm of their own breathing.

Then, with one final breath to steady her nerves, Davi gave the signal.

"Now!"

They rushed forward as one, a blur of determination and steel.

The clearing erupted into chaos. Alexander hurled bolts of flame from behind the jagged cover of rocks, the firelight reflecting wildly in his wide eyes. Will darted low and fast, using the shadows to strike at weak points in the giants' massive legs. Jasper stood as an immovable wall, his shield gleaming as he deflected blow after blow, countering with precision strikes that rang against the giants' thick hides.

Davi and Elara moved in perfect sync, weaving between the colossal swings of the giants' spiked clubs. Davi's sword arced through the air, slicing into one giant's exposed flank, while Elara's arrows found their mark in the joints of its shoulders and knees.

The first giant roared in pain and toppled forward, its club slipping from its grasp. Jasper stepped in for the finishing blow, driving his longsword into the giant's chest with a sickening squish.

"One down!" Jasper shouted, his voice strained.

But there was no time to celebrate. The second giant let out a deafening bellow, swinging its massive club with renewed fury. Davi dodged, rolling to the side and scrambling to her feet, but the sheer force of the swing knocked her off balance.

"Elara!" she called, but when she glanced to her side, her heart skipped.

Elara was no longer beside her. Instead, she was darting around the giant with a speed and grace Davi hadn't seen before. Her movements were almost . . . feral. She leapt onto a jagged rock, propelling herself higher to fire a barrage of arrows into the giant's neck.

Davi staggered upright, clutching her sword. Her limbs ached, but she refused to stop. With a determined growl, she charged back into the fray, her blade carving through the air. The giant was slowing now, its movements more erratic as blood poured from its wounds.

The giant froze mid-swing, its enormous eyes going wide and blank. A deep, wet crack echoed through the cavern as blood gushed from its skull. The beast swayed, and Davi's instincts screamed at her to move. She dove out of the way just as the giant's body crashed to the ground, the impact shaking the earth beneath her.

Coughing through the rising dirt, Davi struggled to her feet. Her vision blurred as she swiped at the air, trying to make sense of what had just happened.

And then she saw him.

Standing atop the fallen giant was a man clad in gleaming silver armor, his presence commanding and terrifying. He yanked a massive halberd from the giant's skull, the blade slick with blood, and rested it casually on his shoulder.

The dust began to settle, revealing his face, but there was no mistaking him from his posture.

Davi's stomach dropped. Her pulse thundered in her ears.

"Charles," she whispered, the name tasting like ash in her mouth.

His piercing eyes locked onto hers, and his expression curled into a cold, familiar smirk.

19

T hrough ragged gasps, Davi's locked eyes with the icy blue depths of Charles's. Hatred surged in her chest, igniting a fresh wave of energy that coursed through her exhausted body. His smirk widened, curling with smug delight. Her stomach churned.

Charles flicked back his golden hair with an air of calculated arrogance. Behind him, his team emerged from the shadows of the forest. The Darkbane Order radiated malice, each of them a figure carved from the darkness.

Davi glanced over her shoulder at her own companions. Jasper leaned heavily on his shield, his armor dented, but his glare unwavering. Alexander's fingers twitched as he narrowed his eyes. Will stood a few paces back, his twin daggers drawn, his eyes darting like a hawk searching for weakness. Even battered, her team emanated a fierce determination.

They had endured impossible odds before. They could endure this too. Especially with Elara.

But would she stay at her side? Doubt flickered like a cold ember in Davi's mind. Elara still had her own reasons to win these Games—and her old team was here now. Could she resist their call?

Davi forced the thought down, gripping her swords tighter. Elara wouldn't fight against her. Not after everything they'd been through. Not after—

"Eleanor, Eleanor," Charles called out mockingly, stepping over the fallen giant's corpse without so much as a glance. His gaze slid to Elara, sharp and predatory, making Davi's skin crawl.

"It's Elara, actually," Elara corrected, stepping beside Davi. Her chin lifted, defiance gleaming in her eyes. The dim light caught her golden hair, giving her the look of a queen preparing for battle.

For a moment, pride warmed Davi's chest, a fragile spark against the storm brewing around them.

Charles' smile widened, his eyes glittering with cruel amusement. "I've been using our tracking stones, and I must say, you all have had quite the adventure," he drawled. "There were times I thought you would fail to get this far." He turned fully to Elara, his voice taking on a razor-sharp edge. "But you've proven your plan was flawless—integrating yourself with this . . . group, letting them do the legwork"—he waved a dismissive hand at Davi, as though she were a mere pawn on his board—"and then delivering them to us so we could take their key after going around the labyrinth and simply waiting here at the gates for it."

Davi's stomach dropped. The words cut deeper than she wanted to admit. Her chest burned with anger, confusion, and a rising dread.

She turned to Elara, her heart pleading to see the denial in her eyes. "Tell me he's lying," Davi demanded, her voice cracking.

Elara hesitated. Just for a moment, but it was enough to send Davi's stomach to her feet.

Charles laughed, the sound hollow and chilling. "I see it, you know," he said, his smirk twisting into something darker, more knowing. "The way the mark is changing you. I'll admit, I underestimated how much control you've gained. Impressive, really, for someone who hasn't drowned yet."

Davi froze. With stomach churning, she asked, "What do you mean, 'for someone who hasn't drowned yet'?"

Charles' smirk deepened, his gaze locking onto Elara like a predator toying with its prey. "Shall we tell her, Eleanor? Or do you prefer to keep your secrets?"

Elara's eyes flared with defiance as they narrowed at him. "Don't," she hissed, her voice sharp enough to cut.

Davi seized the moment, her voice steady despite the storm building in her chest. "I know about her curse," she said, throwing the words like a gauntlet. She hoped to shake Charles, to show him Elara had trusted her. She was with them now. But behind her, Alexander shifted uneasily, and guilt gnawed at her. She'd kept Elara's secret from the others. There hadn't been time. It wasn't hers to share.

Charles chuckled darkly, savoring the tension. "A curse? Is that what she told you?" He leaned in, his tone dripping with mockery. "Oh, it's much more than that. She's Demona-touched, bound by blood magic. A spark of their power already burns within her. She's one of them. Or will be soon, perhaps by the next new moon. It was her idea to use her 'gifts' against you."

Davi's breath caught. Her mind raced to the mark Elara had shown her in the pit, the one she'd claimed was a curse. She had read about the creation of Demonas in her monster-hunting research and suddenly the memories clicked into place: the way Elara's haunting song had cut through the Demonas' lure, her immunity to their magic. Her vision blurred, the world tilting as his words sank in. "No," she whispered, her voice trembling. She turned to Elara, searching for denial in her face.

Elara stepped forward, her hands raised in desperation. "Davi, please, let me explain—"

"You let me tell you—" Davi choked out, her swords faltering in her grip. Memories flooded her mind, now tainted with betrayal: Elara's voice soothing her fears, her touch grounding her, her lips intoxicating her. None of it was real. It was all a lie.

Jasper moved to her side, his shield raised protectively. His tone was steel. "Step away from her," he ordered, his eyes locked on Elara.

"Oh, Dav," Alexander's voice whispered from behind her.

"I knew there was something off about you," Will snarled, daggers gleaming as he edged closer.

Charles raised a hand, and his team moved forward in unison. Davi's eyes flicked to the five figures now fully visible: Igor, the Isavarian witch, his gaze averted; Henry whose sorrowful expression made Davi bristle with resentment; Lucian, the grim Revira priest, arms crossed, calm and patient; Aldric, the hulking brute, tapping his axe in his hand, and Selene whose hungry smirk promised bloodshed.

Charles took a measured step forward, his voice brimming with self-satisfaction. "Though her little tricks served us well in this competition, we will free her from the Demonas' grasp. With the defeat of the dragon, we'll join the Alliance. I'll be the first Tykerial Guardsman to bridge the divide between the two groups. And with that status, we will recover the Healing Stone. We will be heroes. Something you and your ragtag group could never dream of." He gestured dismissively at Davi. "So, why don't you save yourself any further humiliation and hand over your key?"

Davi's knuckles whitened on her swords. She couldn't look at Elara—not now, not with everything crumbling inside her. Elara had never been on their side. She had been a fool to believe otherwise.

But she wasn't about to give up. Not now. Not ever.

"You'll have to take it from my cold, dead hands," Davi spat, stepping forward as she raised her blades.

"Charles . . ." Henry stepped closer to his friend, his tone a warning. "You said we would handle this without violence."

Charles sighed theatrically, his mock exasperation only deepening Davi's unease. "I did hope that would be the case. But it seems they want a rematch," he drawled, his eyes gleaming with cold amusement.

"If this is how you want to play it, you should know we came prepared," Selene's voice slithered as she stepped forward and produced a set of black, gleaming cuffs.

Davi's confidence faltered. Obsidian. Her stomach dropped. "Where did you get those?" she demanded, her voice faltering.

"Connections," Charles replied smoothly, his tone almost bored.

The cuffs—illegal, rare, and devastating—gleamed in the fading light. If Davi or Alexander came too close to them, they would be without their magic.

"You know we'll win. We have before," Lucian said, his tone cool. "Turn back now, and we won't have to use them. Remember, out here, there are no healers, no non-lethal rule."

"Please, don't make them hurt you. He won't be merciful," Henry's eyes begged. His creased brow insulted Davi.

Davi tightened her grip on her swords, her muscles screaming with exhaustion, but her resolve unshaken. "And neither will I," she spat, her voice laced with defiance.

Charles sighed again, shaking his head as he advanced. "So predictable." With sudden, brutal speed, he lunged forward, his boot slamming into her chest. The impact knocked her breathless, her swords clattering to the ground.

Jasper's roar shattered the brief stillness. He charged like a storm, slamming his shield into Charles and sending him sprawling. Charles rolled to his feet, his expression darkening as Selene and Lucian flanked Jasper.

Before Davi could regain her breath, a sturdy rope snapped around her torso. Elara, her face a mix of guilt and resolve, yanked Davi backward.

Chaos erupted around them.

Igor's hands rose, the air shimmering as he summoned a howling vortex. The gale ripped through the battlefield, sending Alexander and Will scrambling to stay on their feet. Loose stones shot upward, jagged and relentless, forcing them to dodge or block with frantic precision.

Davi's attention was pulled back to Jasper as he fought like a cornered beast. His longsword forced Charles back, but Selene darted in, her daggers slicing like vipers. Jasper blocked her, leaving him open for Lucian's mace to crash into his shoulder. He stumbled but roared, deflecting Selene's next strike.

"Cowards!" Jasper roared, raising his shield just in time to deflect Selene's attack.

Charles grinned darkly. "You didn't expect us to fight fair, did you?" He lunged forward, his halberd carving a shallow gash across Jasper's leg.

Davi screamed in frustration, her heart twisting as Jasper faltered. She writhed against Elara's grip, desperate to break free. He wouldn't hold out much longer—not against all of them.

And she wouldn't let him fall. Not while she stood.

Davi reached deep within herself, summoning the magic that simmered within. It surged through her like wildfire, untamed and feral, as she focused on her enemies.

The magic obeyed her silent commands. A wave of crackling energy exploded from her chest, disintegrating her restraints and flying toward their adversaries. The force struck Lucian, knocking him off his feet and forcing Selene to stumble backward and drop her daggers. Jasper straightened, relief flickering across his face as the immediate threat subsided.

But Charles didn't retreat.

His eyes narrowed, then they widened with realization as he took in the raw glow of her magic.

"Another witch," Charles hissed, his voice sharp with disbelief.

His gaze snapped to Elara, who stood frozen, holding the burnt ends of the rope. He gave her a pointed look and motioned his head toward Davi.

"I guess we both have surprises," Davi responded with a smirk of her own.

A flicker of annoyance crossed his face, his lips curling into a snarl. Then he moved with a deadly precision. His halberd gleamed as he advanced, his eyes locking on Jasper again instead of her.

Jasper's longsword clashed against Charles's halberd in an explosion of sparks. Charles kept coming this time. Attack after attack. Each strike of his weapon came with brutal precision, the blows forcing Jasper to retreat step by step. But he held his ground, his shield a solid wall between him and death.

Davi grabbed her fallen swords and darted toward Jasper. Aldric charged at her with a thunderous roar, his massive axe swinging in a deadly arc. She ducked low, her swords slicing upward to counter. Sparks flew as her blades glanced off the axe's haft, the force of the clash sending her stumbling backward.

"No move, witch!" Aldric bellowed, his voice booming. He swung again, the sheer power of his strike carving a deep furrow into the ground as Davi narrowly rolled away.

Henry stood at the fringes of the battlefield, his lute trembling in his hands. Sweat beaded on his brow as he surveyed the chaos. He flinched as Igor's magic crackled nearby.

"Henry, do something useful!" Charles barked, his voice sharp.

But Henry's face twisted with guilt as Davi staggered, barely avoiding Aldric's assault. "I didn't sign up for this . . ." he murmured, his hands trembling as he clutched the lute.

Aldric swung again, this time in a broad horizontal arc. Davi ducked low, feeling the weapon slice through the air inches above her head. She spun on her heel, darting to the side, using every ounce of speed she had to escape his relentless pursuit.

Her focus shifted, locking onto Jasper as he faltered under Charles's renewed assault. A halberd strike slipped past his guard, grazing his arm and forcing him back.

Davi's chest burned with determination. The battlefield blurred around her, every sound muffled but the pounding of her own heartbeat.

"Get away from him!" she shouted, her magic sparking to life once more.

Charles turned, his smirk widening at the sight of her. "Back for more?" he sneered, readying his weapon.

But Davi didn't falter. The magic pulsed in her veins. She raised her hand, energy crackling at her fingertips and fury surging through her veins as her focus sharpened on Charles.

Charles's eyes widened. Fear and worry etched on his usual smug features. But then he shifted—just slightly, just enough.

The spell left Davi's fingertips, a streak of untamed energy tearing through the air toward him. At the last second, Charles twisted out of the way.

Jasper stood directly in its path.

Davi's entire body stiffened. She grabbed a hold of the magic with desperation, trying to stop the blast, to pull it back, redirect it, anything.

But the magic struck Jasper squarely in the chest. His body jerked violently, his longsword falling from his hand as he stumbled backward. The force of the blow sent him crashing to the ground, motionless.

"No!" Davi cried, horror surging through her. She lurched toward him, desperation driving her steps—but before she could reach him, Elara's arm slammed into her chest. The blow sent a sharp jolt through Davi's body, knocking her off balance and forcing her swords to clatter to the ground.

Before Davi could recover, Elara was on her, her expression steely with purpose. In one fluid motion, she snapped the obsidian cuffs around Davi's wrists.

The shackles locked with a chilling click. The connection to her magic vanished instantly, as if something vital had been torn from her. A wave of nausea hit her, making her stomach churn and the world tilt dangerously. Davi gasped, her knees buckling as an exhausting weakness seeped into her limbs, leaving her trembling and unsteady. The obsidian seemed to pulse against her skin, its touch cold and oppressive.

"Elara, don't—please!" she choked out, her voice cracking as she swayed under the weight of sickness and despair. "Let me get to him . . ."

Elara's face twisted with conflict, but she stepped aside.

Davi tried to stand, but the cuffs felt impossibly heavy, her limbs sluggish and uncooperative. She collapsed back to the ground, panic surging as Charles closed in on Jasper. "No! Jasper!"

Charles grinned darkly and swung his halberd with brutal precision. Elara flinched and made a half-step forward, her hand lifting as though she might intervene—but it was too late. The blade struck Jasper's chest with a sickening *crack*, splitting through his armor. The crunch of bone followed—a visceral sound that made Davi's stomach churn.

Jasper let out a ragged cry of pain, and Davi's own scream tore through the air. "Jasper!" Desperation eclipsed all reason as she tried to summon her magic, clawing at the emptiness where it should have been. But the cuffs smothered it, leaving her power silent and unreachable.

"Charles!" Elara snapped, her voice sharp with shock and anger. "That wasn't—" She stopped herself, but her eyes betrayed her disbelief, flicking between Charles and the blood spreading across Jasper's chest.

Davi crawled toward him, ignoring everything else. "Jasper, stay with me," she whispered, her hands trembling as they hovered over his injuries. Her vision blurred with tears.

"Davi, behind—!" Alexander's warning was cut short as Igor's wind magic surged. A jagged stone struck Alexander's temple, and he dropped, unconscious.

Before Davi could act, Aldric's massive hand grabbed her collar and hauled her back. She thrashed wildly, but his knee pinned her to the ground, driving the breath from her lungs.

"Don't make this even harder," Elara said softly, standing over her. There was regret in her voice, but it was buried under resolve.

"Let me go!" Davi snarled, tears streaming as she fought against Aldric's hold. For a moment, guilt flickered in Elara's eyes, but she turned away, joining Charles with a steely expression.

"I'm sorry," Elara mouthed, her lips trembling.

Davi froze at the silent apology, her mind racing. The roar of Igor's vortex abated and she lifted her head to see Will sprinting toward her, shouting her name. But an arrow struck the ground in front of him, halting his advance.

Elara's bow was already drawn with another arrow aimed at Will's chest. "Stand down," she commanded, her voice like ice.

Will hesitated, his dagger trembling in his grip. But he knew better than to test her. Slowly, he sank to his knees, his eyes burning with defiance.

The battlefield fell silent. Davi's chest heaved as she looked to Jasper's still form beside her. Relief came in the faint rise and fall of his chest—he was alive. Barely.

The Darkbane Order stood triumphant, their smirks gleaming in the grim light of their victory.

Charles stepped forward, his halberd resting casually on his shoulder, the polished weapon gleaming ominously in the dim light, still dripping with Jasper's blood. "Well, that was fun," he said, his voice laced with mockery. "Thank you for making this far more entertaining than I expected." With a lazy tilt of his chin, he gestured, and Aldric hauled Davi to her feet.

A lump rose in Davi's throat, her chest tight with helplessness. Tears burned behind her eyes and trickled like streams of lava down her face.

Charles approached with a smirk, his eyes gleaming with cruel triumph. Without a word, he grabbed the chain around Davi's neck and yanked it free. The metal key glinted in the light, a brutal reminder of how close they had been to victory. He turned and strode toward the iron gates, holding the key high before slotting it into the lock.

Aldric let go of Davi and she crumpled to the ground. Scrambling, Davi crawled to Jasper's side, letting the tears fall as her hands pushed through the dirt and blood to get to him. The cuffs rattled on her wrists as her hands shook, hovering over him. There was so much blood. She didn't know what to do.

She looked up when a burst of light and a low, grating creak filled the air as the gate swung open, revealing a shimmering portal to the dragon's ruins beyond. Charles turned back to the Darkbane Order, his voice filled with smug satisfaction. "Come on, let's claim our prize."

One by one, they filed through the gate, their laughter trailing behind them like this was just another day at the tavern.

But Henry lingered, not taking even a step toward the gate.

"Henry," Charles barked, impatience coloring his voice. "What are you waiting for? We're done here."

Henry hesitated, his lute strapped awkwardly to his back, his eyes darting to Davi, then to the gate. "I'm not going," he said finally, his voice quiet but resolute.

Charles turned, a cold sneer twisting his lips. "What do you mean, you're not going? We've won."

Henry's jaw tightened. "You said we'd be heroes, Charles. But this?" He gestured to the carnage around them. "This isn't what heroes do."

Charles let out a sharp laugh, a sound devoid of warmth. "Heroes win, Henry. That's what matters." He stepped closer, his voice dropping into a growl. "Stay here with the losers if you wish. But don't expect any glory when we return as the victors."

Henry didn't respond, his gaze steady. Charles snorted and turned away, stepping through the gates without another glance.

Elara followed behind him, but paused at the threshold. Her expression was unreadable as she turned back to Davi. For a moment, their eyes met, and something flickered in Elara's gaze—a shadow of regret, or perhaps a longing that she couldn't fully mask.

She pulled her emerald necklace from her neck and tossed it at Davi's feet. "To remember me. I hope you find your way back to me someday," she said, her tone light but layered with meaning. Her brow furrowed with sorrow before she turned and stepped through the gates.

Davi stared after them, her chest hollow as the portal's light began to fade. The gate creaked closed with finality, the heavy clang reverberating through the air.

It felt like the weight of the world settled onto her shoulders as the realization hit: all her dreams of happiness, all her hopes of victory—they were gone, sealed behind the iron gates.

Even as the gates to her dreams slammed shut forever, Davi found she could hardly care. Jasper lay in a pool of his own blood beside her.

20

The sobs came unbidden, ripping through her chest with the force of a storm. She hovered over Jasper's still form, his cracked and bloodied armor glinting darkly under the dim light. The moon gleamed above them as the sun's light disappeared under the horizon.

"Jasper!" she choked, her voice breaking as tears blurred her vision. "Jasper, please!" Her trembling hands gripped his cold, slick armor. His face was pale, his breaths faint. But when his eyes fluttered open, her heart soared. Hope surged through her, wild and desperate.

This was her fault. She'd put him in danger; led him here to this.

"Jasper," she whispered, her voice thick with the lie, "you're going to be all right." Blood spilled from his wounds, soaking the earth beneath him. She tore fabric from her shirt, pressing it hard against the worst of them. "Alex!" she screamed, her voice raw. "Alex, come here! Bring the potions!" He had to have some left. He had to.

Jasper's eyes flickered again, his gaze finding hers. His lips parted, his voice barely a breath. "Dav . . ."

"I'm here," Davi promised, sliding closer to cradle his face in her hands. Her fingers trembled as she stroked his cheek. "We'll get you out of here. Just hold on." She poured all her conviction into her words, refusing to look away.

But Jasper shook his head weakly. "It's . . . too late," he gasped, his breath hitching with pain.

"No," she insisted, her voice breaking.

"It's all right." His lips curved into the faintest smile. "It's all right."

Tears streaked her cheeks. "Why did you—" Her voice broke, but she didn't need to finish the question. She already knew the answer. Jasper had acted to protect her—just as he always had.

When Charles had kicked her, Jasper hadn't hesitated. He never did. He had always been her shield, standing between her and the worst of the world. If she'd ever confessed the full truth about what happened in her village, he would've razed it to the ground on her word alone. He would have given her everything.

And yet, she had never crossed that line. She hadn't been brave enough—or strong enough—to accept the love he offered so freely. She hadn't pushed him away, but she hadn't embraced him either, terrified of what it would mean to lean into something so vast, so unshakable.

And now, he was dying for it. For her.

His hand trembled as he reached up to rest it on hers. "You'll win this," he murmured, his voice growing fainter. "You've never . . . given up on what you desire. Don't stop now."

"I can't," Davi sobbed. "This is my fault! I don't deserve—"

"You do," Jasper interrupted, his gaze steady despite the pain. "When you found me in that tavern, you reminded me there was more to fight for. You gave me a reason . . . to believe again. Don't let that go. Keep fighting—for both of us."

"But I can't do this without you," she whispered, tears spilling anew.

His smile deepened, just a fraction. "You must. Don't fear who you are. You're . . . capable of more than anyone realizes." His eyes fluttered shut again, his breath shallow. "Remember the moonlight, Davina. I lo—" The words faded as his head lolled to the side, his hand slipping lifelessly from hers.

"No," Davi whispered, the denial clawing its way out of her throat. "No!" She flung herself onto him, clutching his head as if sheer willpower could keep him tethered to life. She would have given anything—her dreams, her future, her very soul—for the Healing Stone. Anything to bring him back.

Sobs racked her until she had no tears left. She clung to him, mourning not just Jasper but the life they'd lost in the span of moments. The Games and its glory were gone, evaporated like a cruel mirage. So was Elara—her soft touch, her kiss, the bond Davi thought was growing there. And Jasper's steady presence, his unwavering protection. All of it was gone.

When the tears finally dried, her grief turned to bitter dread. Without Jasper, they had no chance. They couldn't win the Games, couldn't stay in the city. She would have to return to the village. There was nowhere else to go. She'd thrown away the man who loved her, ignored what he offered until it was too late.

And now, she had truly lost everything.

A hand rested gently on Davi's shoulder, but she didn't stir.

She opened her eyes to see Will standing over her, his face uncharacteristically solemn. The usual playful spark in his expression was gone, replaced by apprehension and something deeper—grief. It startled her; she hadn't thought his face capable of such emotion.

Will knelt beside Jasper, murmuring the words of the Akarian death rite. Her throat tightened. Jasper was truly gone.

Grief crashed over her like a tidal wave, pulling her under. She barely registered Will's voice until a single word cut through the haze:

". . . brother."

Dread pooled in her stomach. Alexander.

She reluctantly scrambled away from Jasper's lifeless form. How long had it been since Alexander had gone down? Too long.

"Alex," she whispered, fear trembling in her voice. She hurried toward him, before stopping abruptly. Her eyes darted to the bulky charcoal-colored cuffs weighing down her arms. They made her feel weak and nauseous, and the thought of bringing them closer to Alexander twisted her stomach.

"I can't help him," she choked out, turning to Will. "Please, help him."

"That's what I was trying to tell you," Will said gently, stepping toward her. "I need to get those cuffs off you, but—"

"I can help," another voice interrupted from the shadows.

Davi turned sharply, her scowl darkening as Henry emerged. His curly hair was tousled, but his colorful doublet remained almost pristine, an odd contrast to the battlefield's chaos.

"Stay away from us," Davi snapped, her voice sharp with fury.

"It's all right," Will said, his tone soothing. "I've known Henry a long time. He's not like the others."

Davi's eyes narrowed. "Forgive me if I'm not ready to trust anyone else from the Darkbane Order." The sting of Elara's betrayal still burned fresh in her chest.

Will nodded. "I'll work on the cuffs. The longer they stay on, the worse you'll feel." He pulled out a lockpick and knelt beside her.

Henry, undeterred by her hostility, stepped forward, holding out bandages and a small vial of healing potion. Davi hesitated, watching him carefully. She couldn't deny that he'd been different from the others. He had followed the rules in the arena, hadn't joined the fight against them, and had even refused to go with his team for the final battle with the dragon. Still, trust didn't come easily—especially not now.

Her gaze hardened. "Fine. But if you hurt him . . ."

"I know," Henry said softly, his tone steady.

Davi gave a terse nod and held out her shackled wrists to Will.

Henry knelt by Alexander, working quickly to patch up his wounds. Davi's eyes never left him, her body tense and ready to strike at the first sign of betrayal.

Will examined the cuffs, his fingers deft as he began picking the lock.

"You've gotten people out of cuffs before?" Davi asked, her gaze flickering to Henry.

Will smirked faintly, his confidence returning for a moment. "Plenty of times."

"What happened to you?" Davi asked bluntly, her tact dulled by exhaustion. "I mean, I know Selene had something to do with it, but how did a noble's son end up knowing how to disarm traps, pick locks, and break into places?"

Will's smile faltered, his hands pausing briefly before resuming their work on the cuffs. "There's not much to tell, really," he said, his tone subdued. "I'm the youngest son in my family, and somehow, I was always a disappointment. A rebel from the start. While everyone in my family always chose Aurelia, the goddess of air and knowledge, for their patron goddess, I chose Farran, the god of fire and passion. I had big dreams back then—thought I'd be a great musician or maybe a painter." He chuckled softly, almost self-deprecatingly. "Only problem was, I wasn't really good at either. I didn't know who I was or what I wanted to do. Then Selene came along."

He continued working on the lock as he spoke, his voice growing quieter. "We'd grown up together. She was . . . everything. Fun, wild, full of life. We started seeing each other in secret, and for the first time, I felt like I had a place. I wrote her songs, and we spent our time doing all the uncouth, scandalous things we could imagine. She made me feel alive. And for a while, it was enough."

Davi watched him closely as he continued, his hands steady even as his words wavered.

"My father eventually had enough of my nonsense. He wanted me to marry the most boring girl in all the land. I refused. Told him I wanted Selene. He said if I chose her, I'd lose everything. Be disowned." Will's lips twitched with a bitter smile. "I didn't care. I went to Selene, thinking we'd run off together, but . . ." He exhaled sharply, the memory clearly cutting deep. "I found her with Charles that night instead. She didn't even hesitate. She chose him."

He glanced up briefly, his gaze distant. "That was the last time I spoke to her. I was cast out of society and left to make my own way. Turns out I was pretty good at the criminal stuff—breaking locks, avoiding traps, all of it. I suppose that was my real calling all along." His grin returned, faint but defiant, as the lock clicked, and the obsidian cuffs fell away with a dull clang.

Davi felt a rush of relief, as if the chains had been wrapped around her very soul. She hadn't realized how much the cuffs had suffocated her, how they had weighed down her breath and drained her strength. Energy surged back through her body, and with it, her magic.

She turned to see Alexander stirring, his eyelids fluttering open. Relief surged through her chest, only to be swiftly followed by guilt. Her gaze shifted to Jasper's lifeless form.

"This is all my fault," she whispered, her voice trembling. "I trusted her. I put her above all of you. And now . . . this." She looked up at Will, her shoulders sagging under the weight of her words. "You chose the wrong team after all."

Will sighed, shaking his head. "She manipulated you. Besides," he added softly, "it was my idea to trust her in the first place. We never see the worst betrayals coming."

Davi let the words settle over her. "We'll return with nothing. We've lost everything."

Will shrugged, the movement slow and deliberate. "It was never about money for me. Not really. It was more about revenge, fame, maybe a little glory to rub in their faces. But now . . ." His expression softened.

"Now?" Davi frowned, incredulous.

Will met her gaze, his voice low but steady. "I've seen what I've spent my whole life chasing. You are deeply loved, Davi. You might not see it, but it's true."

Her brow furrowed, skepticism shadowing her face.

"Not by me, don't worry," Will added with a wry grin. "But by your brother. By Jasper. They've seen you at your worst and still believed in you. Fought for you. Loved you." His voice softened further, a rare vulnerability showing. "That's more than most people ever get."

Davi's chest tightened at his words. Jasper's love and belief in her weren't something she could dismiss. Even now, with him gone, it lingered like a warm ember in her heart, urging her forward.

"He wasn't wrong to protect you," Will said gently, his tone unwavering. "And he wasn't wrong to believe in you."

Davi swallowed hard, her gaze falling to Jasper's still form. His words echoed in her mind. He'd told her to let go of the past. To embrace who she truly was.

Jasper was gone, but his love remained, etched into her very being. It was time to honor it. Time to own every part of herself—the good and the bad—and fight for the future he believed she could build.

21

A radiant portal burst into existence out of nowhere, its blinding light casting long shadows across the clearing.

"The losers' portal," Davi realized bitterly. The Alliance had prepared it—a way for the defeated to return to the fortress when they realized they had lost. The gates to the ruins were sealed now, closed forever.

Silence fell as everyone stared at the portal, despair settling over them like a suffocating fog. It was over. Truly over.

"Time to go, I guess," Will muttered, his voice hollow.

We'll have to find another way to make this dream work, Davi thought, the weight of it already exhausting her. *A different way to stay in the city.*

Her eyes wandered to where Elara had left her—abandoned and kneeling in defeat. She spotted something glinting in the dirt and leaned down to pick it up. It was the emerald necklace Elara had cast at her feet. Davi had noticed the gem on Elara before, dismissing it as a simple trinket. But now, as she turned it over in her hands, she saw the faint swirl of magic in its depths. Peering closer, Elara's face shimmered into view.

Anger surged in Davi's chest, sharp and hot. Through the gem, she could see the ruins and the battle that ensued—the Wulverns and Zomes scattered like broken toys, the dragon looming above it all.

"A final taunt," Davi hissed. "She wanted me to see her triumph."

But something flickered in her mind. Her eyes turned to the shining portal, then back to the gem in her hand.

A portal spell usually required a memory of the destination—but what if seeing the place through the enchanted gem was enough? Her heart quickened with sudden excitement. She looked to Alexander, who lay sprawled on the ground, his arms flung out dramatically.

"Come on," she said, striding toward him. "Get up. I need your help."

Alexander turned his head to her with a groan. "What's the point? We've lost. Jasper's gone . . ."

"Jasper will always be with us," Davi said firmly, cutting through his despair. "Now get up."

"There's nothing left here," Alexander said, his voice unexpectedly sharp. "The Darkbane Order will defeat the dragon and we will return with nothing. Everything we worked for is gone."

"There might be a way to go after them," Davi said, leaning closer, her voice barely above a whisper.

Alexander's brow furrowed. "Go after them? The gate's sealed."

"What if we can make a portal?" she asked, her tone brimming with quiet determination.

"A portal?" Alexander repeated, skepticism mingling with faint hope.

"What are you two whispering about?" Will cut in, his tone sharp with impatience. "Come on, we need to leave."

Davi ignored him and strode toward Henry, the pendant clenched tightly in her hand. She held it out for him to see, her voice firm and demanding. "What can you tell me about this? Do you know anything about the enchantment on it?"

Henry blinked at the gem, then frowned as recognition dawned. "It's a tracking charm," he said after a moment. "Igor enchanted it to keep tabs on Elara. Charles has the other half and through it they could see where one another was."

Excitement lit Davi's eyes. "I think I can use this to get us to the dragon's ruins."

Henry's gaze lingered on the pendant, his expression thoughtful. "Elara handed you a way in," he murmured, his voice tinged with awe. "She really does care about you."

"Elara did no such thing!" Davi shot back, her tone sharp. "She doesn't care about anyone but herself. She clapped me in obsidian cuffs!"

Henry smiled, his voice soft but knowing. "But she did give you a way in. She left this—her half of the pendant—so you could track Charles."

Davi's brow furrowed, skepticism etched across her face. She remembered Elara's last words to her: "I hope you find your way back to me someday." Could this be what she intended all along? "But if she wanted us to follow her, why would she leave with them in the first place?"

Henry's expression darkened with sadness. "You were outnumbered," he said softly. "She was probably worried for your life. But if you show up at the dragon's ruins, there's still a chance. Elara knows what she's doing, she just needed time. I'm certain she has Aldric's ear. He really only cares about defeating the dragon anyway. It's his life's mission to defeat as many as he can. With those two on your side, you could turn the tide just enough."

Will chimed in, his voice filled with a grim sort of certainty. "Lucian won't turn on Charles, and Selene might seem unpredictable, but she's no fool. She thrives in chaos, but that doesn't mean she's reckless."

Henry nodded at Will, a shadow passing over his face. "If Selene senses she's in danger, she'll do whatever it takes to protect herself. She'll walk the line, playing both sides, but she won't truly cross it unless there's no other way."

Will's jaw tightened. "But let me make one thing clear—if it's up to me, Selene won't even have the chance to switch sides."

"They won't all turn," Davi said, shaking her head. "They can't. They don't win by switching sides."

"No," Henry agreed. "But when it comes to survival, people make choices they never thought they would. If you can convince them that following you is their only chance to live, even Igor might betray Charles."

Davi gripped the pendant tighter, her resolve hardening. If there was even the faintest chance to reclaim what they had lost, she would take it. But this time, it all fell on her. The Streaks on her arms pulsed, a dark hunger awakening beneath her skin. She would have to embrace the part of herself she had always tried to suppress—the part tied to pain, to memories of her abuse. But she would rise above it. Her past would not take this victory from her.

They deserved this win. They had fought too hard, sacrificed too much.

Alexander stood slowly, a faint smile tugging at his lips. He nodded, a glimmer of hope returning to his eyes. "You can overpower Charles," he said quietly. "I know you can."

But when Davi's gaze fell on Jasper's still form, the sharp ache in her chest returned, cutting through her resolve like a blade. She knelt beside him, her voice trembling as she spoke.

"We can't just leave him here," she whispered.

Henry stepped forward, his voice kind but steady. "I'll stay with him," he offered. "I'll make sure he gets back to the Alliance. We'll arrange a proper funeral. He deserves that . . . and I'd like to write a song about his bravery."

Davi nodded, her throat too tight for words. Slowly, she leaned down and brushed Jasper's forehead with a trembling kiss. Her voice broke as she whispered into his ear, "I've always loved you too. I'm sorry I couldn't tell you sooner." Gently, she draped a cloth over his face, ensuring Xevron wouldn't take his soul before the rites could be performed. Tears streamed unchecked down her cheeks, but she forced herself to rise.

Her grief would have to wait. There was still a fight to be won.

Davi held the pendant tightly in her hand, its emerald glow pulsing in time with her quickening heartbeat. Through its depths, the moonlit forest came into view—a fleeting, bouncing image as if seen through Charles's own eyes. Stone ruins loomed in the shadows, their jagged edges softened by the silver light. Charles was running, the uneven rhythm of his movement shaking the image.

Davi turned to Alexander, her voice urgent. "Tell me the words. What's the spell?"

Alexander hesitated, wincing as he held his head, but he forced himself to concentrate. "It's not just the words," he said, his voice tight with effort. "You have to feel it. You need focus. Precision. You're reaching for the place in your mind where the magic is pulling you. Watch the scene—it'll guide you."

"Just give me the words," Davi insisted, her hands trembling slightly.

Alexander nodded, his voice steady despite his exhaustion. "*Misavotive incantare.*"

Davi repeated the words under her breath, the syllables heavy on her tongue as her magic stirred. It had been so long since she'd wielded this much power with intention. It was hungry, wild, rushing to the surface like a dam about to burst.

She closed her eyes and focused on the image in the pendant. The moonlight. The trees. The ruins. She let the hunger of her magic flood her senses, pouring her will into the spell.

The magic burned at first, searing its way through her veins as if testing her resolve. But as she continued the incantation, it began to shift—its touch becoming smoother, more soothing, like a river flowing into familiar channels. She was in control, but only barely.

"You're doing it," Alexander said, his voice breaking through her concentration. "But it's unstable."

Davi opened her eyes to see a bright, circular tear forming in the air before her. The edges wavered and sparked, glowing with a silvery-blue light. Through it, she could see the forest from the pendant—closer now, clearer. The portal strained against her hold, flickering like a flame in the wind.

"Keep going!" Alexander urged. "Don't stop now!"

Davi gritted her teeth and dug deeper into the well of power within her, commanding the portal to solidify. The air around her crackled with energy, the sheer force of the magic making her hands shake.

The portal's edges smoothed into a glowing ring of light. But Davi could feel it—it wasn't steady. It pulsed and twisted, like it might tear itself apart at any moment.

"Go now!" Davi shouted, stepping toward it.

"It's not ready," Alexander warned. "It could collapse any second!"

"We don't have a choice!" Davi shot back. She reached for him, her grip firm on his arm. "We go now, or we lose!"

The ground beneath them trembled as the portal wavered, sparks flying from its edges. They didn't have time to hesitate.

She watched as Alexander and Will dove through the portal before following behind them.

The sensation was like being pulled through a rushing tide, the world spinning and stretching around them. For a terrifying moment, Davi thought the portal would spit them out into nothingness. But then, with a blinding flash of light, they landed hard on damp forest ground.

Davi staggered to her feet, her head spinning as she looked around. The air smelled of earth and rain, the moonlight filtering through the dense canopy above. Stone ruins rose in the distance, just as they had appeared in the pendant.

She turned and watched as the portal she created blinked out of existence.

"We made it," she breathed, half in disbelief.

"Couldn't have made that any more terrifying, could you?" Will asked as he rolled onto his back.

Alexander groaned, pulling himself upright. "It's not over yet," he muttered. He gestured toward the ruins. "We've still got a big bad monster to defeat."

Davi nodded, clutching the pendant tightly as she steadied herself. The magic still thrummed within her, wild and restless. She couldn't afford to lose control now.

"Let's go," she said, her voice resolute. Together, they started toward the ruins, the promise of victory—and danger—waiting ahead.

22

The forest pulsed with the sounds of battle—shouts, roars, and the crackle of fire cutting through the night air. Davi crept through the trees, her breath quickening as the noise grew louder. The glow of flames flickered through gaps in the canopy, casting wild, dancing shadows across the undergrowth.

"This way," she ordered, her voice sharp with urgency. She led the others forward, her pulse thrumming in time with the distant cacophony of combat.

As they emerged at the edge of the forest, the scene before them was chaos. In a wide clearing surrounded by shattered stone columns and rubble, a massive dragon dominated the battlefield. Its golden scales caught the light of the flames it had unleashed, turning it into a terrible beacon of destruction.

The dragon let out an earsplitting roar and swept its tail through a cluster of stone columns, sending them sprawling like children's blocks. Lucian screamed as the beast snapped its jaws, narrowly missing him, and Igor was thrown into the remnants of a crumbled wall by the force of the dragon's wingbeats.

Charles stood at the center of the battlefield, the Alliance's alagon sword in his hand now. He shouted commands that were barely audible over the noise. His usually composed demeanor was gone, replaced by a frantic energy as he tried to rally his scattered team.

"Hold the line!" he bellowed, pointing his blade toward the dragon. "Keep it distracted!"

But his words carried little weight now. The battle was no longer under their control—if it ever had been. The dragon's roars drowned out his commands, and the ground shook with every step it took. Charles's team was being pushed back, their formation breaking as fear took hold.

Davi crouched low in the bushes, her eyes narrowing as she took in the scene. "They're losing," she murmured to Alexander.

He nodded with wide eyes. "He can't get close enough with that blade. He's too afraid."

Charles clenched his fists, his frustration palpable. He gestured toward Selene, who came into view just in front of them, with a crossbow in hand. "Get Aldric and circle around! We need to pin it down!"

Selene hesitated, glancing at the dragon as it unleashed another deafening roar. For the first time, Davi saw fear flicker across her face.

"They're cracking," Davi whispered.

Davi turned to Will, ready to formulate a plan, but he gave her a sly grin. "Selene's mine," he said, already unsheathing his dagger.

"Will, wait—" Davi began, but he was already gone, melting into the shadows.

From their hiding spot, Davi and Alexander watched as Will moved like a ghost through the chaos, closing in on Selene. She stood with her back to him, her crossbow slung over her shoulder as she directed Aldric. Will struck fast and clean, slicing through the strap of her crossbow before she could react.

Selene spun, her eyes flashing with fury as her weapon clattered to the ground.

"Ah yes, there's the face I've been dying to see," Will taunted, his dagger glinting in the firelight.

Selene hissed, drawing a curved dagger from her belt. "You should have stayed in your gambling den," she snarled.

The two circled each other, their movements quick and fluid, like predators sizing each other up. Selene struck first, her blade slicing through the air, but Will sidestepped with ease, countering with a precise thrust.

"Just take her out," Alexander muttered beside Davi, his voice tight with frustration. "If he doesn't hurry, we'll all end up as dragon fodder."

Will was relentless, deflecting Selene's attacks with calculated precision. His dagger flashed, catching her blade and sending it flying from her grasp. She staggered, and with a swift, brutal motion, Will knocked her to the ground.

Davi held her breath as Will knelt over Selene. For a moment, she thought he might finish the job, but instead, he delivered a swift blow to her temple, knocking her unconscious.

Davi nodded to her brother, her expression resolute. "Time to move. Stay close."

Davi started forward, only to freeze as a towering figure emerged—Aldric, his massive axe gleaming like molten silver in the firelight. He loomed over her, his wild eyes burning.

She instinctively reached for her power, magic sparking at her fingertips. She braced herself to strike, but Aldric surprised her by lowering his weapon.

"Elara said you come," he rumbled, his voice deep and rough, like a landslide. "You save us."

"Elara?" Davi's heart leapt. "Where is she?"

Aldric's expression didn't soften, but his axe rose as he pointed toward the battlefield. "Come. We take down dragon." Without another word, he charged, his massive frame hurtling toward the dragon.

Davi sprinted after Aldric with Alexander at her side, dodging through the chaos of the battlefield. The air was thick with the acrid stench of smoke, and the dragon's earsplitting roars echoed off the ruined stone columns. Flames licked the edges of the clearing, casting a flickering orange glow over the massive beast. Its scales gleamed like molten gold, impervious to the arrows and spells ricocheting off its impenetrable hide.

Davi's eyes scanned the battlefield, locking onto Charles as he backed away from the dragon's lashing claws. His movements were sharp and deliberate, ducking behind a fallen pillar as he clutched the alagon blade—a blade of glowing blue-green metal, its surface shimmering.

Her stomach twisted. That sword was the key, their only chance to pierce the dragon's defenses. Without it, they had no hope of claiming the scale that would earn them the win.

"We need that blade," Davi growled, her voice low but firm. "I'll have to take it from him. You stay here."

Before Davi could form a full plan, Will stepped forward, twirling his glinting daggers. "I'll keep him distracted," he said with a sly grin. "You get the sword." And he was gone in a flash.

Her heart pounded as she crept closer. Charles barked frantic orders to his team, his voice tinged with desperation.

Will struck. He appeared behind Charles like a ghost, his daggers flashing in a vicious arc. Charles spun just in time, deflecting the blow with a sharp clash of steel.

"How?" Charles snarled, his eyes narrowing as he parried another strike. "How did you get through the gate?"

Will smirked, his movements quick and fluid. "You've got bigger problems than figuring that out."

Charles sneered, his sword slashing in a deadly arc. Will rolled out of the way, but not quite fast enough to dodge the swing completely. The sword's edge scraped across his arm, sending him to the ground in pain.

"Fool. Do you really think you can take me?" Charles asked smugly.

Davi seized the opening, sprinting into the fight with her sword aimed at Charles's exposed flank. He turned at the last second, their blades meeting in a shower of sparks.

"Ah, Davi, of course you're here too," Charles said with a mocking grin. "Come to play hero again? I almost missed you."

Her jaw tightened, fury burning in her chest. "That sword doesn't belong to you, Charles."

"And you think it belongs to you?" He laughed, the sound sharp and grating. "I'll bury you with it before I let you take it."

Before she could retort, Aldric charged with a roar, his massive frame barreling into Charles and sending him sprawling. Charles hit the ground hard, the sword skittering away.

Davi didn't hesitate. She reached out, her magic surging through her veins as she summoned the alagon blade. The glowing weapon flew into her grasp, its weight solid and humming with power.

Charles froze for a moment, his eyes widening in shock—and anger.

But before she could revel in her small victory, Igor appeared from the shadows, his hands moving in a blur as he chanted a spell. A crackling wave of energy surged toward her, wrenching the alagon blade from her grip and sending it spinning across the clearing.

"No!" Davi shouted, her heart sinking.

In that split second, Alexander sprang into action, stepping in front of Davi with a fierce growl. His hand shot out, deflecting the next blast of energy Igor aimed at her. The force of the magic hit his shield instead. "Get the blade! I'll take care of Igor," he shouted.

Davi hesitated only for a heartbeat, her heart hammering, before she bolted toward the blade.

Behind her, she heard the crackle of magic as Alexander and Igor clashed, but her focus remained on the blade. Her fingers brushed the hilt just as a shadow loomed over her.

"Davi! Watch out!" she heard her brother yell, but it was too late.

The dragon's massive tail swung with bone-crushing force. She rolled onto the ground, but it smashed into her anyway, lifting her off her feet and hurling her across the battlefield. She hit the ground hard, pain exploding through her side as the world spun around her.

Through the haze of agony, she saw Charles staggering toward her, the alagon sword once again in his grasp. He loomed above her, his face twisted with triumph, his shadow long and ominous against the firelight.

"You never learn, do you, Davi?" he said, his voice cold and venomous. He raised the blade high. "This ends now."

Time seemed to slow. Her body screamed in protest as she tried to summon her magic, but her strength was fading fast.

Then came the whistle of an arrow slicing through the air.

23

C harles jerked back, his expression twisting in shock as the arrow buried itself in his shoulder. He staggered, his grip faltering as blood seeped from the wound, staining his armor.

Davi blinked, her vision sharpening enough to make out Elara standing at the edge of the battlefield. Her bow was drawn, the string taut, her blazing eyes locked on Charles. She was ready to shoot again if necessary. Determination radiated from her like an unyielding flame, unshaken even as ash swirled around her like ghostly shadows.

Charles collapsed to his knees, the alagon sword slipping from his trembling grasp. Blood and dirt streaked his once pristine face, his teeth bared in a snarl of fury and disbelief.

"Elara . . ." Davi whispered, hope igniting in her chest even as pain raked through her body like claws.

Elara's voice rang out, clear and commanding. "Get up, Davi! The dragon is yours to defeat!"

Her words burned through the haze of agony clouding Davi's mind. She gritted her teeth and reached deep within herself, summoning every ounce of strength she had left. Her hand trembled as she gripped the hilt of the alagon blade. The moment her fingers closed around it, a surge of heat flared through her body—hope, fury, and determination coalescing into one unrelenting force.

The ground trembled beneath her feet as she staggered upright, the weight of the sword in her hand both a burden and a promise.

This wasn't over.

"How dare you strike at me!" Charles spat, his voice crackling with venom as he glared at Elara. Fury burned in his eyes, but beneath it was a sharp edge of desperation. "You will regret this—you will turn into a Demona!"

"Shhh," Elara retorted, her tone cutting and dismissive. She didn't even spare him a glance. "I'm busy."

With a quick, confident smirk at Davi, Elara broke into a sprint toward the dragon looming at the heart of the battlefield. Its massive wings unfurled like a stormfront, blotting out the sky. Fire glowed faintly in its throat, the light spilling from its jagged teeth and casting an eerie radiance across the shattered ground.

The beast roared, its cry like thunder, shaking the earth beneath them. Stones cracked, the ground buckling as its talons gouged deep into the soil.

"Elara, wait!" Davi called, panic edging her voice. But Elara was moving fast, her bow singing as she loosed arrow after arrow. Each shot streaked toward the dragon with deadly precision, striking its scales with sharp bursts of light. Yet the arrows glanced harmlessly off its armor, the beast barely flinching.

Davi cursed under her breath, scanning the battlefield. She caught sight of Alexander and Will closing in, Alexander's hands swirling with arcane energy as he chanted a spell, and Will flitted between shadows, his daggers glinting as he closed the distance. Igor was nowhere to be seen; Alexander must have dealt with him.

Davi's grip tightened on the alagon blade, the ancient metal humming with power in her hand. With a burst of determination, she charged forward, the blade's green glow cutting through the gloom.

"Fools!" Charles's voice rang out behind her, sharp and desperate. "You think you can win? That dragon will tear you apart!"

Davi didn't stop. The sound of his words faded into the chaos as she surged ahead.

Beside her, Alexander's voice rose in a resonant chant, shimmering barriers springing into existence to shield their approach.

Ahead of her, Aldric let out a feral battle cry, his massive frame barreling toward the dragon. His great axe shining with reflected firelight. He swung with a roar, aiming for the dragon's legs, but the beast reared back, its talons swiping in a deadly arc.

Will darted forward, slipping past the dragon's claws with a dancer's grace. His twin daggers flashed in quick, precise strikes, aimed at the tender joints of the creature's legs. The dragon snarled, jerking its limb back as the blades found their mark, but it was far from slowed.

Elara was relentless, her arrows streaking toward the dragon's head as she ducked and wove through the battlefield. Each shot was aimed for its eyes or the soft tissue of its mouth, but the beast's head shifted too quickly, its fire-lit maw snapping with predatory ferocity.

Davi pushed herself harder, every muscle screaming as she raced forward with her teammates. The alagon blade pulsed in her hand, urging her forward. This was the fight she'd been waiting for.

The dragon turned its blazing gaze on her, molten eyes narrowing as its jaws parted. Fire flared in its throat, the glow intensifying as it prepared to unleash destruction.

And Davi, gripping the blade with all her strength, kept running.

Her focus locked onto the dragon, its massive form wreathed in heat and shadow. The blistering fire it unleashed surged forward in a torrent, and Davi raised her free hand instinctively. With a cry, she summoned a freezing wave of ice, the spell streaking toward the flames. The elements collided in an explosive burst of steam, the battlefield briefly shrouded in a swirling, hissing fog.

The clash gave her a moment to breathe, but as the vapor thinned, the truth struck her with brutal clarity. The dragon's fire was relentless, a force of destruction that even her magic and Alexander's combined couldn't hold back forever. And her companions' steel was useless against the beast's armored scales.

Her grip tightened on the alagon blade, its weight anchoring her in the chaos. This sword was their only hope—the only weapon capable of piercing the dragon's impenetrable hide. But the realization dawned on her with chilling finality: it couldn't be her wielding it.

Magic affected the dragon more than the steel blades, wearing it down, opening opportunities. Her role wasn't to strike the killing blow, but to unleash the power surging through her veins and clear a path for the one who could.

She exhaled sharply, her heart pounding. She would have to let go.

She glanced at Elara, who was weaving through the chaos with the precision of a huntress, her bow firing rapid volleys that kept the beast's attention divided. Elara moved with grace, courage, and purpose. In that moment, Davi understood. Elara was the one who could strike the killing blow.

Her heart twisted, not with doubt but with something far more profound: trust.

"Elara—take the blade!" Davi shouted, her voice cutting through the roaring flames.

The dragon twisted violently, its tail smashing into the ground. A shockwave of dirt and debris exploded outward, forcing Elara into a desperate dive to avoid the strike. Dust clung to the air, but even disoriented, Elara never faltered. She rolled to her feet, firing an arrow at the dragon's head. The beast snarled, snapping its jaws, the shaft splintering harmlessly against its armored scales.

"Elara!" Davi yelled again, her voice breaking as urgency overtook her. The dragon's claws raked the earth, carving deep furrows as it lunged toward Elara, its molten gaze locked on her.

The realization hit her like a blade through her chest. The fiercest battle she was fighting wasn't against the dragon or the shadows of her past. It was against the walls she had built around herself, the fear of relying on anyone else. And now, here in the heart of the battlefield she gave in to the relentless fire of a love she never saw coming.

"Catch!"

Davi thrust the alagon blade forward and channeled her magic into a surge of wind. The spell propelled the sword, spinning through the air like a green comet, straight toward Elara.

Elara glanced up, her eyes widening for only a fraction of a second before her hand shot out. She caught the blade mid-roll and rose to her feet, the blade gleaming in her grasp.

And for the first time, Davi felt the fire of trust burn brighter than her fear.

The battlefield stilled, the air humming with tension as Davi stumbled back, summoning another blast of ice as the dragon shifted its full attention toward Elara.

The dragon roared and lunged, its massive claw slicing through the air with terrifying speed. Elara leapt to dodge, but the beast's strike was too fast. The claw caught her mid-motion, its brutal force sending her hurtling backward. The alagon blade slipped from her grasp, clattering to the ground as her body crumpled against an outcrop of stone.

"No!" Davi's scream tore through the battlefield.

The dragon's molten eyes locked onto her now, its massive head lowering as its maw opened wide. Fire churned in its throat, a blinding, searing light that promised annihilation.

Davi raised her hand just as the inferno surged toward her. Her shield spell flickered into place, a shimmering barrier of light that caught the full force of the flames. The heat slammed into her with brutal force, her knees buckling as cracks began to form in the spell.

The air was thick with smoke and ash, choking her lungs and stinging her eyes. Her arms trembled violently, the strain of holding the barrier pushing her to her limit. Flames licked at her legs, searing through her torn armor, and the edges of her magic frayed, the shield flickering dangerously.

"Hold on!" Alexander's voice echoed faintly through the chaos, a desperate plea barely cutting through the roar of the dragon.

Her focus narrowed, every ounce of her will pouring into the trembling shield. She couldn't falter—not now. Her vision blurred as sweat and blood streamed down her face, and each breath came in shallow, ragged gasps.

The dragon halted its fire, allowing a brief respite.

Then, through the haze, she saw it all—everything, all at once.

The dragon reared above her, its molten eyes blazing, one massive claw raised high, poised to deliver a crushing blow. Elara lay crumpled against the rocks, blood staining her side as she struggled weakly to rise. Alexander and Will were nearby, battered and staggering, trying in vain to find a way to distract the beast. Aldric's battle cry faltered as he swung his axe with desperate strength, only for the dragon's tail to whip around and send him crashing into the ground.

The alagon blade glimmered faintly, lying abandoned and far from Elara's reach.

And then, there was Charles—his twisted smirk cutting through the carnage as he dragged himself upright, his eyes gleaming with malice. He was watching, savoring their impending defeat.

The weight of it all crashed down on her. They were losing. Charles had been right, they were going to die.

Something deep inside her snapped.

With a raw, guttural scream, Davi thrust her hands forward, abandoning her magic shield and unleashing the unbridled fury of her magic. A violent storm of lightning and shadow erupted from her, a chaotic torrent that struck the dragon mid-lunge. The beast howled, its momentum shattered as the magic tore into its flesh, coiling around its massive frame like serpents of pure destruction. Scales cracked and peeled away under the assault, and the ground trembled beneath its thrashing body.

But the power wouldn't stop.

The magic poured out of her, wild and unrelenting, scorching everything in its path. The air crackled with energy, smoke rising from the blackened earth at her feet. Her veins felt as though they were on fire, the searing intensity threatening to tear her apart. She staggered, her body trembling under the weight of the force she had unleashed.

Darkness crept into the edges of her vision, a shadow that wasn't hers. A DarkHeart. She could feel it rising within her, whispering promises of endless power, its insidious pull dragging her closer to the abyss.

"No . . . no! I have to . . . stop!" she gasped, her voice a fractured plea. But the magic roared louder, a beast of its own, untamed and hungry. It clawed at her soul, threatening to devour her completely.

"Davi!"

A voice cut through the chaos, sharp and desperate. Then a hand gripped her shoulder, firm and steady, anchoring her to reality. She turned, her wild, tear-filled eyes locking onto Elara's.

Elara stood bloodied and battered, her body shaking with exhaustion, but her gaze was fierce and unyielding. Despite the blood on her lips and the tremor in her voice, she spoke with commanding clarity.

"You've done enough," Elara said, her voice breaking. "Let it go. Please. I can't lose you—not like this."

Davi faltered, the words hitting her like a hammer. Elara stepped closer, and before Davi could protest, she pulled her into a desperate, trembling embrace. The contact was grounding, the warmth cutting through the icy pull of the darkness clawing at her mind.

"Elara . . ." Davi choked, her voice raw and fragile. Her magic fought her, raging against her will, but Elara's presence was like a beacon in the storm.

"Come back to me," Elara whispered, her grip tightening.

With a final, primal scream, Davi wrenched the power back, dragging it from the world and forcing it deep within herself. The darkness recoiled, its tendrils snapping as she severed its hold. The magic vanished in an instant, leaving behind silence so heavy it was deafening.

The dragon collapsed with a thunderous crash, its lifeless body striking the ground and sending a tremor through the battlefield. Smoke and ash swirled in the air, mingling with the cries of relief from her companions.

Davi slumped to her knees, her body trembling, her breathing ragged. Elara knelt beside her, not letting go, her arms still wrapped tightly around her.

"You're here," Elara murmured, her voice soft, a fragile relief breaking through.

Davi nodded weakly, her body trembling with exhaustion. Tears streaked her soot-stained face, and her lips twitched into a faint, tired smile. "We . . . did it . . ." she whispered, her voice barely audible over the stillness that had settled after the chaos.

"You did," she said, her voice soft but filled with conviction.

Elara hesitated, the weight of unspoken words pressing heavily on them. Slowly, she loosened her hold on Davi, though her hand lingered in hers. "I'm sorry," she began, her voice cracking. "For before . . . for leaving. I didn't want to."

Davi tried to respond, but her body was too drained, her words caught somewhere between her heart and her lips. She closed her eyes as darkness began to creep into the edges of her vision.

"Elara . . ." she whispered, her voice faint.

"I'm here," Elara said quickly, leaning closer. "I've got you. I'm not letting go this time."

The warmth of Elara's touch anchored her, even as the exhaustion pulled her deeper into the void. The battle was over, but its scars—the visible and the unseen—would be theirs to carry.

And in that fragile silence, as her body surrendered to unconsciousness, Davi found solace in the steady presence of Elara by her side.

24

D avi woke in a grand bedroom, a soft canopy above her came into focus.
The air was thick with the soothing scent of incense and herbs, a faint
shimmer of magic lingering where healers worked diligently with potions and
whispered incantations. By her bedside stood Alexander and Will, their faces a
mixture of exhaustion and relief.

Alexander's shoulders relaxed visibly as her eyes fluttered open. "Davi," he
murmured, his voice laced with both worry and relief.

"What happened?" Davi croaked, her voice hoarse, her mind foggy. Memories
danced just out of reach—fragments of light, pain, and the surge of her magic
tearing through her.

Will's gaze hardened, and he motioned for the healers to leave. They bowed
silently, retreating from the room to leave the three of them alone.

Alexander perched on the edge of the bed, taking her hand gently. "You scared
the living shit out of me!"

Will smirked at Alexander proudly. "A proper curse! Finally!"

Alexander smiled despite his serious tone and rolled his eyes. Then his voice
softened as he began to explain. "Your magic exploded, and you took down the
dragon. Then Elara . . . she hacked off a dragon scale with the alagon sword and
placed it in your hand. She backed away, and everything happened so fast."

He took a breath before continuing. "The portal appeared. The Guardian
Alliance came through to greet the winners."

"They were surprised to see both teams in the final arena," Will interjected,
leaning against the wall with his arms crossed. "It's not against the rules or
anything, but I bet it will be next year."

Alexander nodded. "The Fangslayers were named champions. Afterward, we were all brought to the Guardian Alliance's fortress to recover before the ceremony tomorrow."

Davi sat up straighter, the weight of his words settling over her. "Where's Elara?"

Alexander rolled his eyes, his tone dripping with sarcasm. "Oh, we're fine, by the way. Thanks for asking."

A smile tugged at Davi's lips as she swatted his arm playfully. "Well, I can see you're fine."

Will sighed, his expression a mix of irritation and amusement. "Elara's with the losers, I assume. The Darkbane Order will be at the ceremony too, collecting their . . . second-place award, or whatever."

Alexander leaned closer, his expression softening. "Davi," he said quietly, his voice full of awe, "we did it. You did it. You led us through the entire Hunt. We're the winners of the Games."

The weight of his words filled the room. Alexander's next words were almost a whisper. "We don't have to go home now. Ever."

Davi blinked, letting the thought sink in. A swell of pride and relief bloomed in her chest—but it was short-lived. A shadow crossed her face as another memory clawed its way forward.

"Jasper's body?" she asked, her voice trembling.

Will and Alexander exchanged a look before Will spoke. "Henry kept his promise. He brought Jasper through the other portal." His tone softened, though the sorrow behind his words was unmistakable. "His body is being prepared for the funeral rites. He'll be honored as a Fangslayer with us tomorrow and then his funeral will take place tomorrow night."

Davi nodded slowly, her throat tightening. The thought of never seeing Jasper's easy smile, never hearing his laugh, or feeling the steadiness of his presence again cut through her like a blade.

Will stood, his movements deliberate. "We'll let you rest," he said, glancing at Alexander, who followed suit. "We need to be ready for tomorrow."

Davi watched her teammates—the remnants of her team—file out of the room, their footsteps fading into the quiet. For a moment, she stayed where she was, staring at the closed door. The silence felt oppressive, thick with the weight of what they had gained—and what they had lost.

Her thoughts turned to Jasper, the ache in her chest sharpening with each breath. She had wanted to win the Games, had dreamed of standing with her team in the halls of the Alliance. But not like this. Never like this. The thought of being here without him felt hollow, as if the victory had come at too great a cost.

Unable to sit still, she moved to the window, drawn by the pull of the stars. Her fingers hesitated before she pulled back the heavy curtains, letting moonlight spill into the room.

The nearly full moon hung high in the sky, its silvery glow washing over the fortress grounds like a soft, ethereal light. The quiet beauty of the night wrapped around her, but it offered no solace. She realized she must have been asleep for at least a day, perhaps more, yet she still felt tired.

Jasper's absence filled the room like a shadow. Davi leaned against the window frame, her eyes on the moonlit horizon. Nothing would ever be the same again.

A soft knock echoed through the room, pulling Davi from her thoughts. She turned toward the door, assuming it was Alexander coming to check if she was resting. But when she opened it, her breath caught.

"Elara," she whispered.

Elara stood in the doorway, a vision of understated beauty. Her simple gown flowed around her like moonlight, and her green eyes shimmered with a mix of hesitation and hope.

"Alexander said it would be all right if I came to see you now. Can I come in?" Elara asked, her voice quiet, almost tentative.

Davi felt her heart lift, the heaviness of the past day momentarily lifting. She nodded quickly, stepping aside to let Elara enter.

As the door clicked shut behind them, Elara turned to face her. She seemed to gather herself, her hands clasped nervously in front of her. "I needed to see you," she began, her words spilling out like a dam breaking. "I wanted to say how sorry I am."

Davi's eyes softened, but she said nothing, letting Elara continue.

"When I left you . . . I thought I was doing the right thing," Elara said, her voice tinged with regret. "What happened to Jasper—I couldn't see that happen to you too. I didn't want to go with Charles, but I knew he wouldn't stop unless I did. I had to get him away from you. I needed time to talk to Aldric, to figure out a way to end this. And I hoped . . . I *hoped* you'd find your way to me."

Her emerald eyes shone with unshed tears as she took a shaky breath. "I'm sorry for so many things. For not telling you the truth about my curse. For keeping so much from you. I know that being Demona-touched makes people mistrust me. It's . . . it's changed me. My voice. My appearance. I can feel it making me more like them every day." Her voice faltered, but she pressed on. "I was afraid it would change how you saw me. How you felt about me."

"Elara . . ." Davi whispered, stepping closer.

"I wanted to protect you," Elara said quickly, her words catching. "But Davi, I . . . I—" She broke off, her lips trembling as the words refused to come.

Davi reached for Elara's hand, her fingers warm and steady, grounding them both. A soft smile touched her lips, and she met Elara's hesitant gaze. "I know what it's like to want to hide part of yourself," she said, her voice low but sure. "Your Demona mark . . . maybe it drew me to you at first. But it didn't make me care for you. Not like this."

Elara's breath caught, her green eyes widening. A shaky laugh slipped from her lips, and she shook her head slightly, her tears spilling over. "You think no one can understand what you're carrying," she said softly. "But you're wrong. I see you, Davi. I see the weight you've had to bear and the strength it's taken to keep standing under it. And I don't care how heavy it is—I'll carry it with you. I'll carry you, if that's what it takes to make you believe this."

Davi's lips parted in surprise, Elara's fingers trembling as she brushed Davi's cheek. "You are more than the monsters in your past, more than the magic they tried to twist. And to me, you are the moonlight cutting through all of it—you are everything."

Davi stared at her, stunned into silence, her heart pounding as the words washed over her.

"Elara," she whispered, her voice cracking, but Elara shook her head gently, silencing her with a small, tentative smile.

"I love you. All of you," Elara said, her voice soft but unwavering.

The words hung in the air between them, delicate and perfect. For a heartbeat, neither moved, as though breathing too hard might shatter the fragile moment. Then Davi leaned forward, her lips brushing Elara's in a kiss that was achingly tender. It wasn't like the wild, desperate kiss they had shared in the dark pit, all raw emotion and fear. This was slower, deeper, filled with promises unspoken and emotions laid bare.

Elara's hands found their way into Davi's hair, tangling gently as she pulled her closer. The warmth of her touch felt like an anchor, tethering Davi to the present, to her.

"I want you," Davi murmured, her voice soft against Elara's lips. "All of you. Always."

Elara let out a quiet, breathy laugh, her hands sliding down to clasp Davi's. "Always," she echoed, her voice steady now, her golden gaze luminous with certainty.

With a gentle tug, she guided Davi to the bed. They sank onto the soft covers together, lying side by side as moonlight streamed through the window, painting the room in silvery light.

For a moment, the world beyond the walls ceased to exist. The pain, the losses, the weight of their battles—none of it mattered. There was only Elara, her touch, and the quiet hum of shared love between them.

But as Elara slipped the silk robe from Davi's shoulders, the moment faltered. Davi stiffened, her breath catching as her eyes dropped to her arms, then her chest. The Obsidian Streaks had grown. They carved their way across her skin in jagged, dark lines—bold, inescapable, undeniable.

Her voice cracked as she whispered, "They've almost taken over."

Elara sat up slightly, her fingers tracing the edges of the Streaks with deliberate care. "They're beautiful," she said firmly, her golden gaze locking with Davi's. "They're a part of you. They don't scar you or mar you. They make you you. You don't need to hide them—not from me, not from anyone. We both have our own marks."

Davi blinked, her throat tightening. No one had ever said that before. The Streaks had always felt like something to cover, something to endure. But in Elara's eyes, there was no pity, no fear—only love.

For the first time, Davi felt no shame in the marks that defined her, no urge to cover them. Instead, she felt an overwhelming sense of lightness, as if a piece of her soul had been set free.

She smiled, the warmth in her chest expanding until it felt like it might burst. Leaning forward, she rested her forehead against Elara's, their breaths mingling in the moonlit stillness.

"I'll find a way to save you," Davi whispered, her voice steady but filled with quiet resolve. "We'll find a way around your curse together. I won't let you turn into a Demona, Elara."

And then Elara kissed her again, deeper this time, letting the moment sweep her away. As the moonlight spilled over them, unbroken and whole, Davi felt a quiet peace settle within her—a peace she had never thought possible.

25

Davi blinked her eyes open, disoriented for a moment as the room came into focus. The fine linens beneath her were soft and luxurious, but they were nothing compared to the warmth of Elara's arms wrapped tightly around her.

For a brief, wondrous moment, she thought she might still be dreaming. She caressed the smooth skin of Elara's arm, letting her fingers trail lightly, as if the touch might anchor her in this reality. She didn't want this feeling to end.

Elara stirred beside her, a soft murmur escaping her lips before she opened her glittering eyes, yawning.

"Good morning," Elara said softly, her voice still husky with sleep. Her smile was gentle, her arms remaining snug around Davi.

"It is a good morning," Davi replied, her lips curving upward as she turned to kiss her.

Elara's smile grew as the kiss broke. "You're getting your medals today," she said, her tone light but proud. "You and your team are going to be solidified into the Alliance. No one's ever made it through the Hunt with just three members."

The word "three" struck Davi like a blade. She felt the familiar pang of loss in her chest, sharp and unrelenting. Jasper. His absence lingered like a shadow, always present. Would it always feel this way?

Without a word, she slipped out of bed, the chill of the air brushing against her skin as she moved toward the chair where her robe lay draped. Sunlight streamed in through the tall window, golden and bright, but Davi found herself yearning for the serene glow of the moonlight from the night before.

She dressed herself in a fine, dark-blue dress, its flowing fabric cinched at the waist, layered beneath a leather breastplate that bore the scars of battle. As she adjusted the armor, she reached for Jasper's Tykos amulet, fastening it carefully to her chest. The weight of it was a quiet reassurance, a reminder that he was still with her in some way.

When she caught her reflection in the mirror, she almost didn't recognize the woman staring back. Her dark hair fell in loose waves, framing her face. Faint cuts and bruises traced her skin, remnants of hard-fought battles; but her green eyes . . . they shone differently now. They were sharper, filled with wisdom and resilience, a reflection of everything she'd endured and overcome.

The long sleeves of the dress covered the dark Obsidian Streaks that had fully overtaken her arms, but she could still feel their presence beneath the fabric.

Behind her, Elara approached, resting her chin on Davi's shoulder. Their reflection in the mirror was striking—a warrior and her golden archer.

"A dress fitting a champion," Elara said softly, her eyes glowing with admiration.

Davi studied their image for a moment longer. She was not just a winner of the Guardian Games. She had also won the heart of this extraordinary woman. How had she gotten so lucky?

She turned suddenly, cupping Elara's face in her hands and pulling her into a kiss. It was full of quiet desperation, of gratitude, of the longing to preserve this moment forever.

When they broke apart, Davi's voice was low but steady. "Everything I've been through—every hurt, every tragedy—led me here. And while I would never wish to be abused or scraping by to survive in this city . . . or to lose Jasper"—her voice wavered slightly, but she pressed on—"I can see now that this was the path that was laid out for me. It's not perfect. I'm not perfect. But it's mine. And I'll walk it with pride."

Her eyes burned with unshed tears as she added quietly, "I'll make Jasper proud."

Elara smiled, brushing a hand gently against Davi's cheek. "I'm sure you already have."

The words settled in Davi's chest like a balm, easing the ache, if only for a moment.

For the first time in what felt like forever, she felt a true, unrestrained smile spreading across her face. As she stepped into the hallway, the sunlight spilling around them, she knew she was ready for whatever came next.

Davi felt a pang of unease as she watched Elara walk away, down the hall in the opposite direction to join the members of the Darkbane Order. She trusted Elara, but after everything, the thought of being apart, even briefly, was unsettling.

A guide led Davi to the grand arena doors. As she walked, Davi couldn't help but marvel at the towering halls of the Alliance's castle. The stone walls were etched with intricate carvings of past champions, and banners in rich gold and crimson hung from the vaulted ceilings. This would be her home now.

The thought sent a shiver down her spine—equal parts awe and trepidation.

She reached the arena doors, where Alexander and Will were already waiting. Her heart swelled with pride as her eyes fell on Alexander. He stood tall in his finely tailored vest adorned with shining gold filigree, his youthful face softened by a growing confidence. The streaks of white in his dark hair were more prominent now, giving him an air of wisdom beyond his years. He looked at ease, something she hadn't seen in him for so long.

Will, always the rogue, wore a sleek black suit with a gray pocket square, his smirk a testament to his usual mischief.

"Well, it's about time you showed up," he teased, his tone light but carrying a hint of mischief. His sharp gaze glinted with amusement. "Busy this morning, were we?"

Davi rolled her eyes but didn't take the bait. Instead, she stepped forward and wrapped her arms around Alexander in a fierce hug.

"Can you believe this, Alex?" she asked, pulling back to look into his eyes.

"You know," he said, his voice steady with quiet pride, "I can."

Her chest swelled with emotion as she looked at the two of them—the remnants of their team, her chosen family. Each of them wore Jasper's Tykos symbol proudly. His spirit was with them, and he would be honored today alongside them, before they lay him to rest that evening.

Will handed Davi the dragon scale, now secured in a satchel. "You should be the one to present it," he said, his voice uncharacteristically solemn.

Before Davi could respond, the massive arena doors creaked open, revealing the roaring crowd inside.

Together, the three of them stepped forward into the large arena. Their carriage awaited, adorned with banners of gold and crimson. They climbed aboard, and the vehicle began to carry them around the edge of the arena.

The crowd erupted into cheers, their voices thunderous as confetti rained down from the stands. Music swelled, joyous and triumphant, as Davi's gaze swept over the endless faces. She allowed herself to feel the weight of their victory, the magnitude of what they had achieved.

Their carriage came to a stop near the grand platform, where the Leader of the Alliance, Peter Stonestride, stood waiting. Davi caught movement from across the stage—the Darkbane Order. Emerging from their side of the arena, they walked to their designated place.

Her eyes immediately sought out Elara. She stood slightly apart from her team, her gaze meeting Davi's with a mixture of pride and uncertainty.

This was the moment.

Davi and her team stepped forward, standing tall before the gathered crowd as Stonestride addressed the assembly.

"City of Gilderon," his voice boomed, carrying over the arena through a tube. "The Games have been completed. The scale has been retrieved, and our warriors have returned home. Only one team holds the proof of their triumph." His sharp gaze scanned the assembled competitors. "Will the team with the scale please step forward and present it?"

Davi hesitated for a moment, savoring the tension in the air. Then she nodded to Alexander and Will, and together they stepped forward as one.

Reaching into the satchel, Davi drew out the dragon scale. Its iridescent surface caught the sunlight, casting shimmering hues across the platform. A collective gasp rippled through the arena, followed by a roar of applause.

Davi raised the golden scale high, her heart pounding as the cheers washed over her.

Peter raised his arms, commanding silence. "Through trials and tribulations, the best team has prevailed! It is no easy feat to win the Games. I declare the winners of the Games . . . the Fangs—"

"No," Davi interrupted firmly, her voice carrying over the platform. "We are the Mighty Four. We will enter the Alliance as the Mighty Four."

Stonestride frowned slightly, his brow furrowed in confusion. "Four?"

Davi's voice remained steady. "I want Eleanor from the Darkbane Order to join us."

The crowd erupted into murmurs, shock and curiosity sweeping through them. Elara's eyes widened, surprise flashing across her face.

Stonestride chuckled, though it was tinged with disbelief. "Well now, that's not really—"

"The Victory Clause," Davi said sharply, cutting him off. "It allows the winning team to bring worthy members from other teams into their ranks. Eleanor Everwood of the Darkbane Order fought valiantly. She has earned her place."

Stonestride looked momentarily taken aback but quickly recovered, a wry smile tugging at his lips. "That clause is ancient. It was put in place to bolster numbers when the Alliance was new."

"It's still in the official rules," Davi countered. "And I invoke it now."

All eyes turned to Elara. The silence was palpable as everyone waited for her response. Charles, her team leader, shot her a glare, his eyes promising retribution. But Elara, with a calm and quiet defiance, stepped forward.

"I accept. But I will go into the ledger as Elara Everwood," she said, her voice clear and unwavering.

The murmurs grew louder, but Stonestride finally relented, raising his hands to quiet the crowd. "Very well. The Mighty Four it is."

The crowd's cheers erupted once more, louder than ever. Davi and her team beamed as they stood together, united under their new name. Confetti and praise rained down on them, but Davi's focus remained on Elara, now standing proudly at her side.

As the Darkbane Order was escorted from the stage, Davi caught Charles's sharp, venomous glare. His lips moved silently, but the words were clear: "You'll pay for this one day."

Davi gave him a sweet, pointed wave, knowing there was nothing he could do now.

This was her moment, their moment, and she wouldn't let anything tarnish it.

Each of them took their turn signing the book. Davina Kusovo. Alexander Kusovo. William Bresolis. Elara Everwood. Their names, freshly inked, were now etched into the history of the Alliance. Stonestride passed the book to an attendant, who carefully stowed it away to rest among centuries of legacy in the guild's library.

Stonestride stepped forward again, a solemn expression softening his commanding presence. "And we honor the fallen as well," he said, his voice carrying through the hushed arena. He unfolded a piece of parchment. "Jasper Thorne. His funeral rites will take place here, in the arena, tonight. May Xevron guide him to his rightful place in the underworld. His name will be etched into the Alliance's fallen ledger as well."

The words hung heavily in the air. Davi swallowed hard, her hand instinctively seeking Elara's. Elara squeezed it tightly, anchoring her as the crowd offered a moment of quiet respect.

When their names were announced one last time to the roaring crowd, Davi's heart swelled with pride and sorrow in equal measure. But as the cheers washed over her, a faint dizziness began to creep in. The edges of her vision blurred, and she blinked hard, willing it away.

It's just all the intense emotions, she told herself.

The victor's parade awaited them, a triumphant procession through the streets of Gilderon. The city would celebrate their success, their survival. But with each breath, Davi felt her strength waning. A sharp, searing pain lanced up her arm, and she clenched her jaw against it.

Not now. Not now.

Her stomach churned, nausea rising like a tide she couldn't stop. She forced herself to keep moving as her team was ushered off the stage, each step heavier than the last.

"I'm fine," she whispered under her breath, a mantra she didn't quite believe.

Her knees buckled, and she stumbled into Alexander.

"Davi?" he said sharply, catching her. His eyes, wide with alarm, searched her face. "Are you all right?"

"I'm . . . finnn . . ." The words slipped from her lips, garbled and faint.

Her legs gave out completely, and she sank to the ground. Elara was there in an instant, her arms wrapping around Davi. The arena fell silent, the crowd's cheers snuffed out in an instant as confusion rippled through the stands.

Davi's hands trembled as she lifted the sleeve of her gown. The black Streaks that crawled up her arm pulsed ominously, throbbing with a deep, unrelenting ache. The sight of them sent a wave of dread crashing over her.

They were getting worse.

Davi clenched her teeth, her mind racing even as her body faltered. She had thought she was free—free to enjoy this victory, free to embrace the life she had fought so hard to claim. But now, there was something new to run from.

If she and Elara were to have any kind of future together, if she was to survive this, she needed to find the Healing Stone. And now she understood, with terrifying certainty, just how fast time was running out.

This wasn't the end of her story. It was the beginning of another fight.

The Games were only the beginning. The story is far from over.

Want to know where destiny takes Davi and Alexander? Continue the adventure in *Obsidian Tide*, the first book in the *Lumos Gems Chronicles*, and uncover a world of rising darkness, ruthless enemies, and a fate long in the making.

ACKNOWLEDGMENTS

Writing a book is never a solitary endeavor, and *Monsters, Moonlight, and Magic* would not be what it is without the incredible support of so many people.

To my mom and dad—thank you for always believing in me, encouraging my creativity, and reminding me that I could be anything I wanted to be.

To my sisters, who let me lead the way and brought my worlds to life first, your support means everything.

To my husband, Scott—your love for stories has pushed me to dig deeper into my own, and I am endlessly grateful for the way you encourage me to chase my dreams. Your belief in me, in my writing, and in the worlds I create has been a constant source of strength and inspiration. Thank you for always being my anchor, my adventure partner, and my biggest fan. I couldn't do this without you.

To Ryan Johnson, who introduced me to D&D and RPGs when I was convinced I wouldn't like them—thank you for proving me wrong. You opened a door to stories I never knew I needed, and for that, I will always be grateful.

To the amazing authors of the *From Loathing to Lovers* collection—Katie, Courtney, Lindsey, Jessa, and Taylor—thank you for welcoming me into this project with open arms. Your support during my first independent publication has meant the world to me. I'm honored to be part of this collection with you.

A huge thank you to Jennifer Robinson, whose insight helped me step back and see what this novella was meant to be and brought the fire of storytelling back to life in me.

To my incredible alpha readers, Susan Shepard and Katelyn Davis—your enthusiasm and thoughtful feedback fueled my own excitement and helped shape this story into what it is now. You both worked so hard on this manuscript, reading some parts over and over again for me, and I can't thank you enough for your dedication.

To my beta readers—Eric Anderson, Jacque Schwartze, Jessica Gonzalez-Smith, Lauren Youree—your thoughtful feedback and encouragement made this story stronger and made me believe in the magic in these pages.

And to my editor, Heather Hudec—your editing style was exactly what I needed. Your keen eye, insightful suggestions, and the way you truly understood this story made such an impact on me. But beyond that, I deeply appreciated your reaction comments throughout your read. Seeing someone who loves and reads as many books as you do react so strongly to this story reassured me that I was on the right track. Your enthusiasm gave me the confidence to trust my instincts, and for that, I am beyond grateful.

To my incredible social media community—thank you for loving this story before it was even a fully formed idea. Your excitement, encouragement, and enthusiasm from the very beginning helped fuel my own passion for this novella. Knowing there were readers eagerly waiting for Davi's story made the entire journey even more special.

Lastly, to you, dear reader—thank you for stepping into this world and following Davi and Elara's journey. I hope you fell in love with them as much as I did.

About the Author

Photo by Carmen Seda

By day, JoAnna works as a software developer, but her true passion lies in weaving enchanting stories that transport readers to magical realms. A lifelong writer, JoAnna's love for storytelling is rivaled only by her love for books and her enthusiasm for fantasy games.

When not lost in the land of Akaria, she's busy connecting with fellow fantasy lovers on Instagram, working on her next novel, or plotting her next adventure with her husband, who helps bring her stories to life.

For updates on future releases, fun extras from the world of Akaria, and other news, visit JoAnna's website at www.joannamcspadden.com.

ALSO BY JOANNA MCSPADDEN

The Lumos Gems Chronicles
Obsidian Tide
Midnight Embers

www.ingramcontent.com/pod-product-compliance
Lightning Source LLC
Chambersburg PA
CBHW050337110726
47899CB00007B/2530